The Boy and the Donkey

The Boy and the Donkey

Life is not a Journey

1ST EDITION, 2021

NESTOR T. KOLEE

Cover: Giovanni Misagrande
Printing: Amazon Media EU S.à r.l., 5 Rue Plaetis, L-2338, Luxembourg
Editing: finetexts, Corina Retzlaff

ISBN: 9798776683374

www.nestorkolee.com

For Vincent and Valentin
So you'll always follow your dreams.

Prologue

The little boy was so proud. He rode on his donkey and led the whole caravan. The other children sat on their animals and followed him. His father had signed him up for the little donkey ride. The man who owned the animals had looked at him and then put him on the lead donkey.

So they rode off, and the boy kept stroking his donkey. The group moved steadily through the beautiful Andalusian landscape. Always ahead was the little boy, who hardly noticed the surroundings and only had eyes for his animal.

They had ridden about halfway when the lead donkey stopped abruptly. He tilted his head a little and began to graze. The little boy was pleased. "Eat properly first," he spoke to his animal. And he did not stop petting him while the donkey rested.

But the other animals had not stopped. The child who was sitting on the second donkey in the group now rode past them. He had always had the little boy in front of him all the way and was now glad to be in front for once. As the child passed the boy, he beamed. The child sitting on the third donkey also rode past them now. So did the fourth and the fifth, and so on.

The little boy, however, kept stroking his donkey. "Just rest a little, you've earned it," he said, smiling. The donkey continued to eat in peace, letting the other animals pass by.

The little boy noticed how the children riding by began to change from time to time. While the first ones were just happy to be a little further ahead themselves, the children riding at the back began to be more and more pleased that the little boy and his lead animal were moving more and more to the end. The joyful smiles had turned first to indifference and finally to a sardonic grin. Some even laughed mockingly and said silly things.

The little boy, however, did not mind. He hardly heard it. If he noticed it, he was only a little surprised. But then he quickly turned back to his donkey, which he had not stopped stroking, and encouraged him to continue grazing. This went on until the last child had ridden past them. On his face, the little boy had seen something like pity because this child knew how it felt to be at the end of the caravan. The last will be first. That's what this child had always been told. But he had long since lost faith in that.

When the last donkey rode past them, the little boy's animal stopped grazing. It lifted its head, looked briefly at the caravan, and then started moving all by itself. As if the little boy's continual petting gave it energy, the lead donkey now ran after the others at his own pace. Thus, as at the beginning of the journey, he was a little faster than the others, and child by child, donkey by donkey, they began to overtake the others again.

The faces of the children looked quite different this time. While the last child of the caravan still seemed to be happy that at least he had not been at the end all the time, astonishment at first spoke from the looks of the others, which then condensed into resentment and envy . Among the children who were still at the front, the little boy sensed something like competition. He thought he noticed that they were trying to urge their animals to run faster so that his donkey could not overtake them. But it was worst with the leader: whereas once there had been a radiance on his face, now anger struck the little boy as he gradually rode past him too.

So the little boy's donkey finally led the caravan again. All this time he had not stopped petting his donkey, and his initial pride had now turned into deep love.

It was drizzling. Light rain fell on the windscreen. The wipers rubbed the few drops with the dusty sand the car had picked up on the Spanish country road. The smeared dirt formed streaks. They blended into the barren wasteland of a leaden, heavy landscape through which Tom steered his car. He had lost his bearings. His whole life no longer offered him any direction.

It had been weeks since his father's death. But with each day that passed since then, this disorientation increased. His father was Tom's only family. Now he had no one. At some point, he couldn't take it anymore. He needed to get out, needed a change of scenery. Maybe that would help. But it didn't help. Tom knew that when he arrived in Málaga. This time away would only make things worse. Because even if the place changed, the disorientation remained.

He had rented a car and just driven away. Questions circled in his head. Questions Tom had still wanted to ask his father, to see more clearly for himself. To find a direction for his life. But death knows no questions and it gives no answers. It leaves everyone alone. Alone in the very nothingness that made up the landscape

Tom was driving into. It was somewhere in the Spanish countryside that seemed as empty as Tom's life.

The last sign pointing to a place to stay was a long time ago. It led far off the main road into the mountains. Tom knew when he made the decision to turn off that his fuel would not last for the return trip. *What was the point of going back either?* Tom thought. *To a life that no longer exists? What sense would there be?*, he thought over and over again. If his father had been alive, he would surely have given him an answer. It would have been the answer of an optimist, because only steadfast optimists always have an answer. Even when life is silent. *What is the point of it?* At that thought, Tom paused for a moment. Wasn't that the central question? *What is the meaning of life, anyway?* Tom would have liked to ask his father at least this one more question.

He glanced beside him at the passenger seat. There lay all that reminded him of his father. It was a manageable sized box, not really big, not really small. Unspectacular, just like his father's life. The box was closed. But Tom had a clear picture in his mind of what was inside.

Inside the box was Tom's heart stone. That's what his father had always called it. It was a small green crystal. Tom remembered exactly what his father had always said to him. *It protects you. When it's with you, nothing can happen to you.* Tom's father had always claimed the stone was a shard of the *Tabula Smaragdina*. The tablet was a myth on which, according to ancient legends, was written the secret of the world's soul. Tom had marveled and treasured the stone. As he grew older, he was increasingly sure it was more likely a washed-out shard of glass his father must have found on the beach once. But as a child he had believed in magic, and he felt that something magical still emanated from that stone. Especially right now, as he thought of his father. It was a spell that kept him alive for a moment. Because his father had possessed this one gift. He knew how to tell stories about the world, and those stories came true. *I miss his stories. I miss him. Father could always make sense of life,* Tom thought.

The rain had become heavier by now, and through the washed-out window of his car Tom could now recognize in the distance the lodging which the sign on the main road had indicated. It was a large, old wooden house, situated at the foot of a wooded slope on the side of a mountain. From a distance it looked as if it had been cut into rock. But as Tom got closer, he realized that impressions were deceptive. The house was built right up against a rock wall that jutted out of the forest. Slippery wooden planks led up the path. As Tom got out of the car, it slowly began to storm and the rain turned more and more into a thunderstorm. From below, the house had looked eerie. It had seemed gloomy, just as if it was from another century. But Tom had no choice. At least there seemed to be light inside. Dripping wet, he finally stood in front of the somewhat warped entrance. Tom hesitated for a moment. Then he saw the strange name carved into the wood above the door and wondered what was possibly waiting for him inside this house.

Chapter 2

Tom was pleased to find that the wooden house was warm and cosy. It seemed to him quite different from what it had looked like from the outside. It was not so gloomy, more like an enchanted place. Tom was greeted by a large room, with a massive iron bowl in the middle. It was attached to the ceiling and hung over a large fire. From it came a comforting warmth that filled the entire room. To his astonishment, Tom was not the only visitor. Scattered around the room sat more than a handful of guests. They were eating and talking. Tom watched them for a moment, feeling as if he were in a special place. *How strange the world is,* he thought to himself. It was the first time in his life that he had set out without a destination or a thought. In the past, he would never have dared to do that. *After all, in life you always need a plan of where you are going, otherwise you get lost,* he had always told himself. *Yet life seems to have a plan of its own and you can follow that too,* Tom thought now as he contemplated this strange place. He still didn't quite know how he had come to be here.

"Why so disoriented, you're here," it snapped him out of his thoughts. A small, motherly old woman suddenly stood beside him. She looked kindly at Tom. "Sooner or later it leads them all here." Tom did not understand. The old woman smiled at him. "The disoriented ones. " She looked at Tom. "They always come to Nepanthé." Tom remembered the strange name he had seen outside. *Nepanthé was* carved into the wooden frame there above the door. *But what was the meaning of that name?* Questioningly he looked at the old woman.

"Just be patient, you'll figure it out. But for now come along, you must be hungry." She led Tom to one of the small tables near the iron bowl. The fire was warm and slowly drying his clothes. Although the place still seemed strange to him, he felt increasingly safe and secure. He was thinking of the old woman's words and the name of this place when the first drinks and food were served. *How strange, I didn't order anything,* he wondered briefly. But then it struck him that he hadn't eaten anything proper for hours. So without asking any more questions, he ate and drank and was glad to finally be able to eat his fill again.

"Do you like it?" Again, the old woman stood beside him. With a smile that only satisfied hunger can induce, Tom looked at her. "It's delicious. I didn't even have to order it, it came naturally." The old woman smiled again, as she had when they first met. "This place knows what you need," she said, and was gone immediately. Tom didn't even have time to think about her last comment, because it wasn't long before she returned. She brought two filled goblets made of plain clay and sat down at the table with Tom.

"This place is named after a potion from Greek mythology." She paused before continuing. "*Nepenthes* was a medicine added to wine to remove suffering, chase away fear, and make one forget all illness. It was a gift from the gods." Tom looked inevitably at the two clay jars as she continued. "It is the purpose of this place to take away the suffering of those who find their way here. The fearful lose their fear, the sick enjoy life again." She paused and looked at Tom with a piercing gaze. "And the disoriented are shown a way." Tom knew she meant him and wondered what that path was. Then she continued, "This place here is called Nepanthé, because that is what it is: a place without worry." Then the old woman fell silent.

A place without worry, Tom thought. Wasn't that what he had been looking for when he had left home a few days ago? A place that would end his suffering and make him forget his pain. "The disoriented always come to Nepanthé?" repeated Tom, questioningly, the phrase the old woman had said at the beginning of their encounter. She looked at him and nodded dumbly. "But I did not come here deliberately. It was the last chance to find a place of refuge. " Again the old woman smiled. "And yet you are here. Or perhaps because of it," she said peaceful.

Tom pointed to his cup. "I have to drink that?" The old woman pointed to her cup too and said, "We'll drink together. But it's your choice. There's nothing in life you have to do if you don't want to." Tom wasn't sure what he should think of that, but he was starting to gain some confidence. He reached out for his cup and asked his next question, "What happens then?" The old woman looked at him with a deep inner calmness, "All worries dissolve." Tom thought. What did he have to lose? She wouldn't poison him. He really had no reason to distrust her. The food had tasted delicious, and she had given him a seat by the fire. The other guests in the room seemed friendly as well. If they also had been drinking from the cup when they came here, it obviously has not harmed them. Probably the drink and its mystical effects were just a figment of the ancients' imagination anyway. Perhaps it was simply an affectionate gesture towards the guests. Surely everybody else had gotten lost as well, as hidden as the place was. Probably nothing would happen. At best he would just have a good feeling again when he went to bed later. Possibly he would be spared a restless night of bad thoughts if he drank with the old woman. "Why are we drinking together?" asked Tom, after thinking that, after all, it was only his worries that were supposed to dissolve. "To connect you with this place," said the old woman. Tom smiled. Probably the old woman just enjoyed drinking quite a bit. He was starting to like the way she talked and seemed to see the world. It reminded him a little of the magic his father had always known to spread by the telling of his stories. *To my father*, he thought as he raised his cup. The old woman did the same and they both drank. It was wine, indeed. It tasted very sweet, but there was something bitter in it too. Tom drank it in one draught, as one drinks medicine. The old woman had also drunk quickly and was already getting up again.

"What now?" asked Tom, seeing that she was going to leave. "I told you that already. Your worries will fall away from you." Tom looked a little disappointed at the old woman. Had she just been joking? He was already getting annoyed by his own simplicity, when the old woman said something else: "Go to sleep now. Your dreams will give you guidance."

When Tom heard this, he knew he had been tricked by the old woman. For he never dreamed. He had not had a single dream since he was a child. What she had said might have made some difference to the other guests. Perhaps they all had been lying in their beds in the evening, completely blissful by the wine, and were telling of their dreams on the next morning. But he knew that wouldn't work for him. He just didn't dream. Tom almost believed he couldn't anymore. As if she had read his mind, the old woman looked at him one last time. In a serious voice she said, "This night you will dream."

Chapter 3

In a distant desert, in timeless space, the Bedouin In Lak'ech sat in the shade of a palm tree and waited. He had been waiting for what seemed like an eternity now, and he knew that waiting was what he was really meant to do. Sitting and waiting. Until something happened. Until something moved in this eternal expanse of grains of sand. Until the same cycle of day and night, sun and moon, until the steady ebb and flow of life was interrupted by something. Until the moment came when In Lak'ech interrupted his entire existence to turn to the task. The supreme task for which he sat here waiting.

The Bedouin sensed that this moment was starting to approach again. He had been watching the sand. For a long time he had watched it. He had fixed his gaze firmly on the desert, sinking into it so that at some point he was one with it. He felt every single grain of sand, felt connected to it, as if a whole world of life was hiding within it. It was a world full of possibilities that lay within the cosmos of a single grain of sand. Only by observing, or as he himself always called it, by not observing the grains of sand closely, could he perceive every single emotion that was going on inside them.

Today he had sensed something again in a tiny grain, in one of those little worlds, far away on the horizon, not visible to the human eye, but clearly and distinctly perceptible to him. Something was going on. Something had moved on the horizon. Only imperceptibly, but clearly. And it would continue to move.

"It's that time again," the Bedouin thought and began to prepare for his task. "Once the question is asked, it always sets something in motion." Be it something as small as a grain of sand. But then, just by that one small movement, it can't help but get bigger. It becomes more urgent. With all its power it seeks an answer that will inevitably lead the questioner to it.

So it was this time, too. What the Bedouin had just perceived as the movement of a small grain of sand on the horizon was approaching him now. A shadow had appeared in the distance. It was a friendly and bright shadow. A person formed more and more from its outline the nearer it got to the Bedouin.

In Lak'ech didn't know any time. It just did not exist in this place. The Bedouin kindly explained to any visitor who wondered that this place was free of the illusion of time. Just as the place was also freed from the illusion of space. And so it happened that the man the Bedouin had been expecting since his first spotting in the sand was suddenly standing right in front of him.

"Nice to see you again," the Bedouin greeted him kindly. "Seems to me it was only yesterday that we saw each other." Inevitably he had to grin at his remark about the word yesterday. Astonished, the man looked at him. "How did I get here?" he wondered.

"You ask that every time," the Bedouin replied, smiling gently. The man did not understand. "Have I been here before?" he asked the Bedouin, for he could not remember.

"It may be hard for you to understand, but there is no time here. Therefore, you were, are, and always will be here, except when you are not," was the only answer In Lak'ech could give. The man was confused, and the Bedouin could see it. *It always feels that way when they are here consciously*, he thought to himself, and yet decided to help the man a little so he could get used to this environment. "Don't even try to grasp it with what you call reason. The easiest way is to feel that you are here and that it is right at this moment." Though the man still didn't understand, those words did have a calming effect on him. His confusion eased somewhat as he stopped focusing his mind on understanding how he had gotten here. He accepted that he was here, in the middle of a desert, in front of this Bedouin, with no idea of beginning or end and no idea of what he was supposed to be doing here.

"Shall we begin?" the Bedouin asked gently. "Begin what?" the man asked. The Bedouin motioned for him to sit down. In front of him, the man vaguely saw a broad and flat object lying on a small table and stretching all over it. A precious ornate fabric covered it, so that he did not know exactly what was underneath. The Bedouin laid his hand on the cloth. "Begin what?" he repeated the man's question. "I think, with answering the question you came here to ask." The man looked at him in wonder. Yes, there was something there. There was an inkling that there had been an important question. A question he had only recently asked himself. A question that had been completely hidden in his life waiting for him until now and had become of all the more pressing importance. He wasn't sure if he was just remembering it or if it was the Bedouin he heard it say. But with the sentence the Bedouin was speaking, it had come back into his reality. "The question of the meaning of your life. The question of what you are actually in the world for. The question to the answer that should give you direction again." The Bedouin looked into the man's eyes and knew that the man finally remembered.

"So, shall we begin?" the Bedouin asked, pointing to the object lying face-down in front of them. "I'm sure this time you'll get quite a bit closer to the answer, my dear Ala K'in." The man listened. It was the first time the Bedouin had called him by a name. *But that's not my name at all,* the man was still thinking as he watched the Bedouin slowly pull the fabric aside.

Astonished, the man looked at the object that appeared underneath. "It is a mind mirror." In Lak'ech looked at the man firmly. "That is why you are here." The man did not understand. A strange feeling spread through him. He had not dared to look at himself in the mirror for any longer. Though he could't tell why not. Only briefly had he looked at the object and recognized it for what it was. The mirror was set in a beautiful frame with rich decorations. They gave it the appearance of something precious and yet simple at the same time. It was a mirror such as anyone might have with them, perfectly ordinary in its way, indeed almost inconspicuous. Yet, the man thought to himself, there was a rarity about the mirror, created by the ornaments and patterns that entwined themselves around the mirror's surface. He tried to look at them more closely. The marvelous thing was that these ornaments seemed to speak a language. As they did so, they spread out and began to grow larger around the mirrored surface. Symbols became visible, written characters. They were words, ancient wisdoms, spreading out and reaching into life. They groped their way in all directions, as if trying to reach the man's ears. "Look at us, Ala K'in," they whispered. Quickly, Ala K'in turned away from the mirror.

"So now you remember your name," the Bedouin smiled at him. The strange feeling that had been spreading through Ala K'in since his first cursory look at the mirror eased his confusion and led to a blissful relaxation. Distraught when he arrived here, he now felt completely peaceful and tranquil by the idea of simply being here. He still didn't know where he came from, but that didn't bother him. Neither did it matter what would be or what he was supposed to be doing here in this strange place. All that mattered was this moment. This exact moment he was in right now. Timeless. Spaceless. Just as the Bedouin In Lak'ech had told him.

"My name is what you call me," he heard himself saying to the Bedouin. Ala K'in had also made peace with his name. The perfect calmness he felt now made him accept what he was given here. Deep down he felt that his name, that names at all and naming things were meaningless. If anything, it seemed to him, they solidified, turned to stone, and were bound to crumble sooner or later. Naming rips things out of the blissful state of being, out of the only moment that really exists, and from the moment Ala K'in was in right now.

"You have learned much since last time," In Lak'ech said, not without some pride, as he watched Ala K'in thinking. "Keep that insight." Ala K'in looked puzzled. "What insight?" Good-naturedly, the Bedouin looked at him, "That there is only this moment you are in. That it is the only one that matters. The moment in the here and now, made so that your here and now can dissolve." Ala K'in didn't know of what use such an insight would be. Still, he could tell from the Bedouin's face that In Lak'ech wanted to make a gift of what he had just said to him. Or perhaps to a weapon, a cloak of protection, or a spell to keep him from the evil.

"How do I find the meaning of my existence?" asked Ala K'in after a while. The Bedouin continued to gaze at the desert. "This place imposes trials upon you," In Lak'ech replied gently and calmly. "If you pass them, you will know the meaning of your existence." Silently, they sat and contemplated the desert. "You said, we have done this many times?" Ala K'in asked after a while. "Yes, my dear Ala K'in, we have done this many times," repeated the Bedouin. "With what result?" The Bedouin looked at him a little mischievously. "Always with a different one." "That means, I have passed the tests before?" Ala K'in asked. "Sometimes yes, sometimes no. One time you found the meaning of life, the other time you didn't even look for it." Ala K'in did not understand. "How is that possible?" "Well, it's just always different. Life is always different." The Bedouin paused before continuing. "But every time you come here, the meaning of your existence can be revealed to you." He listened a little to himself. "But this time I have a good feeling that you will come as far as you ever have been." He looked kindly at Ala K'in. "Shall we try?" the Bedouin asked patiently.

Ala K'in was silent for a moment. He thought a bit about what the Bedouin had told him. Though he was not sure he had understood it all, a tiny residue of the blissful feeling that the fleeting glance in the mirror had given him spread and settled over his doubts. Finally, with a satisfying certainty he took from the moment, Ala K'in asked the Bedouin, "What do I have to do?"

"You have to think," said In Lak'ech in a bright and friendly voice, pointing to the mirror. When Ala K'in looked into it, he gazed upon something that seemed strange altogether. It was the image of a boy riding a donkey.

Chapter 4

Tom startled up. Sitting upright in his bed, he struggled to get his orientation. A storm was raging outside and slowly he remembered where he was. He was still in Nepanthé, the place without worry. After the strange conversation with the old woman, he had been given a room and had fallen into his bed. The potion had made him sleepy. *Had that been a dream?* He was still too dazed to remember fully when suddenly a flash from outside lit up the room. Tom saw himself briefly in a mirror that hung opposite the bed. He was startled. Now he remembered. He had actually been dreaming. For the first time in decades, he had dreamed. Just as the old woman had said. As he was still thinking about what it all meant, tiredness overcame him again and he fell into a deep and peaceful sleep.

When he awoke the next morning, the sun was shining. The birds were chirping and Tom felt he was in the most peaceful place imaginable in the world. When he went downstairs to the big room with the firepot, he felt more rested than he had ever felt in his life.

Some of the other guests were already there and had breakfast. Tom went to his table. The fire had gone out in the meantime, but the sun's rays, which fell into the room from outside through the windows, provided sufficient warmth. The room no longer seemed so enchanted as it had the night before. Instead, it radiated a peace that transmitted to Tom. *The old woman had been right. This place makes one's worries fall away.*

Again, food and drinks were served naturally. Tom was pleased when he saw what was available: fresh eggs with crispy bacon, golden toast, an omelet with ham, peppers, and mushrooms. There were also waffles with honey and fruit, as well as a fresh orange juice and hot coffee. *Who's going to eat all that?*, Tom thought enthusiastically, and found that his appetite was enough for it. As he ate his breakfast, he thought again of his dream. It was a strange dream. Tom wasn't sure if it had been a dream at all for he had forgotten what dreaming felt like. *Yet I guess we have to dream in order to live,* he suddenly thought. *The path of life is only revealed to one in dreams.* He was wondering a bit about these thoughts. Was this a realization from last night? Tom could not tell. Right now it was enough for him that he perceived the world here and now a little more peacefully. It had been quite different at home. There was only his job. It was not a bad job. It covered his existence. In fact, Tom had never thought much about it. Usually, it was part of his life, like the apartment he lived in, like the town he lived in, and like all the other things he did in his life. But since his father's death, times were no longer normal. Just as normality had fallen out of his everyday life, work and everything else could no longer support him when he needed it most. That was when it had started, when everything had started to fall apart after one thought had suddenly entered his life. The moment his father died, a deep, inner voice reminded Tom that life was finite. It whispered it in his ear, became his daily companion, and from day to day and time to time it showed him what his life was really like. And the more it showed him, the worse it got. What he had done silently yesterday, demanded fulfillment today. What he had done thoughtlessly until today asked for meaning now. For trying to find some magic in his life, he was left solely with the green stone and the memory of his father. It was the certainty that this magic was long gone and would never return that slowly ate away his old life. It was so intense that he finally had to flee. It was Nepanthé, this place without worry, where he felt peace again after a long time.

"Did I promise too much?" With a good-natured smile, the old woman stood by his side. She looked very different today. No longer like a gnarled little sorceress witch in her enchanted inn, but like a dainty old fairy who could make the sun's rays of light appear with her wand and grant wishes. Tom was glad to see her again like this and felt an inner attachment. So he also immediately asked her what his dream was all about. "I can only take away your worries," she looked at him with a smile. "I can't interpret your dreams."

She had been gone for a while already, when the landlord came to his table. Tom had hardly noticed him until now. He had assigned him his room the night before and had him paid for in advance. As he stood at his table he whispered to Tom, "There is a dream interpreter not far from here. He can help you understand your dream."

Chapter 5

The path led him even higher into the mountains. The innkeeper had shown him where the way up began not far from the hut. "The dream interpreter has lived up there for many years. Longer than this place has existed," the innkeeper had told him. "He would have known that dreams would come here eventually. That's why he was there even before Nepanthé existed." Tom wanted to know, why he was so sure the dream interpreter could do what he claimed. "Because he interpreted my dream," the innkeeper said. "Without the dream interpreter, there wouldn't be Nepanthé."

It took Tom a while to reach the top. The way was steep and arduous, and Tom kept thinking of his dream. In a timeless desert he had met a Bedouin. He had promised Tom to reveal to him the meaning of his existence. He had called him by a strange name and had spoken of tests which Tom would have to overcome if his destiny was to be revealed. Before he could begin, he had awakened. But there was something else. The picture of a little boy on a donkey in a mind mirror, as the Bedouin had called this object. "You have to think," were the last words of the Bedouin that Tom remembered. What a strange dream. Tom couldn't make any sense of it. He had paused when the innkeeper had told him about the dream interpreter. Did he really want an explanation? But the innkeeper had told him that there were two groups of people who came to Nepanthé. One spent a short time there, dreaming. They enjoyed the inner peace that the place gave them. They enjoyed their dreams, which they did not know how to interpret. Someday, they left Nepanthé, and with the place also their dreams. As children they went back to a life of adults. "For some the sorrows come again, for others they do not. But all forget their dreams in time," the innkeeper had said. "What they are left with is a feeling that sometimes makes them wistful. A feeling, that once there was a dream they should have followed." When Tom asked about the other group, the innkeeper just had said, "They go to the dream interpreter."

The dream interpreter was standing on a hill when Tom had covered the last few yards of the path. Tom recognized him immediately, though he had never seen him before. Everything on him was white. Tom wondered what could have brought him here to the mountains. "Your dreams," he heard the tremendous voice of the wise old man say, now standing right in front of him. "Their powers always attract a dream interpreter." Tom wanted to know why, but he didn't dare to ask a question. He respected this man very much. If the little, motherly old woman had been like the warm earth that gave Tom solid ground under his feet, here he found himself face to face with someone who seemed to guard the heavens and only showed the way to those who proved themselves worthy. *I'm certainly not one of those*, Tom thought. But he had done well to keep silent since the dream interpreter continued to speak. "These powers want to be unleashed. However, most people do not understand how to accomplish this. They know better how to lock in their dreams."

"If I even knew what my dream was trying to tell me," Tom snapped. The dream interpreter looked at him with a stern expression. Then he was silent for a while. "How can you not know, when he already knows?" he said suddenly, pointing to something in Tom's pocket. Tom looked puzzled for a moment, then felt his coat and winced. *There was no way this man could know.* He inevitably reached into his pocket and grabbed the small box containing his heart stone, which he had tucked away into his jacket and carried with him the whole time after he had left the car. *Surely he saw that I was carrying an object. The bulge in my coat pocket must have told him.* Tom became suspicious. *Perhaps he and the landlord were up to no good.* He had probably noticed the little box the night before, which Tom guarded like the apple of his eye. Possibly the landlord had suspected treasure in it, and had now lured Tom here into the mountains so this man could take it from him. *I'm sure he's trying to trick me.*

But the wise man said, "You have to cherish your green stone since it already knows where your path will lead you. It brought you here, and it will lead you on. Now come along." Then he turned away and walked to an old cypress tree that grew on a ledge. Tom's thoughts flashed through his head as he slowly followed the dream interpreter. *How on earth did he know about my stone?* Tom hadn't opened the box since he found it beside his father's deathbed. "For Tom" it said in his father's handwriting on the small note leaning against the box. His father must have put it there for him when he suspected his life was coming to the end. Tom had opened it and burst into tears when he saw the crystal. All these memories of his childhood, everything he associated with his father, who had tried to be both father and mother to him because there was no one else. All the stories and wonders from a time long gone crystallized with their images all at once from that little green stone. It was that moment when Tom's world came crashing down. While holding the box with the crystal in his hands, he felt everything around him collapse. The entire facade of his life began to crumble away. It had been a backdrop he had been safely navigating until that small gust of wind that poked out of the box as he opened it caused it all to collapse. All that was left was sheer disorientation. Tom didn't know where to go with himself or his life anymore. Until he came here. So the dream interpreter had already been right. His stone had led him here. *How could he have known all this?*

"Sit in the shade of that tree," said the dream interpreter, pointing to the old cypress. "I need to listen to the wind." Tom sat down, not quite knowing what to do. After all, he had not even told this man about his dream. Or did he already know this one, just as he had known that Tom was carrying his heartstone?

"Tell me about your dream," the old man asked. Tom told him about the desert and the Bedouin. He told of the tests that had been foretold and of the revelation of the meaning of life. He spoke of the mind mirror and what he had seen. And he repeated the Bedouin's words, "You have to think." When he had finished his explanations, the dream interpreter looked at him in silence for a while. The wind was blowing steadily at this height, and a slight rustling could be heard in the cypress.

"Can you interpret my dream?" Tom asked. Again the wise man was silent for quite a while. Then he said, "It is a particularly difficult dream. Most dreams, on the other hand, are simple. They are simple because they are self-contained and convey a clear message. Your dream, however, is not yet finished dreaming. It has not yet revealed to you everything you need to know. It is an unfinished dream and those are extremely rare." Tom thought about what he had heard. "So can you help me?" he asked, confused. He felt despondency rising within him. *If my dreams are already so complicated, how am I supposed to find meaning in my life?* "We need to talk about my payment first," the old man suddenly said rather seriously. It occurred to Tom that he hadn't even talked to the dream interpreter about the payment for his services. But the way the man said it made Tom suspicious again. *Surely he wants my stone. However he discovered it, he must suspect some great value in it. Perhaps it really is an ancient crystal, as Father had always claimed.* "What do you want?" asked Tom and looked with a serious expression at the dream interpreter. But the latter only smiled before he spoke, "I don't know yet. But when your dream is finished, I will tell you. Whatever it is that I ask then, you have to promise to give it to me." Tom hesitated for a moment. "And if I don't have anymore dreams?" he asked at last. "Then I shall remain without reward, and you will be an eternal seeker," replied the dream interpreter.

Now he's tricked himself, Tom thought. *If I don't like what he says and I don't keep dreaming, I don't have to give him anything. Even if I had another dream, I wouldn't have to go back to him and tell him about it. So what have I got to lose?*

The wise dream interpreter watched Tom and saw his thoughts. *He still carries a lot of distrust from his old world,* he thought. *This is going to be a difficult journey for him.* He paused for a moment. *It's always that way when a journey begins with someone's death. When death sends one on his way, it will come again to claim his reward.* But he preferred not to tell the boy about that. *It is sometimes better if we do not know everything that will happen on a journey,* thought the dream interpreter. *Otherwise we might not begin it at all. Even if it leads us to our destination eventually.*

"Agreed," said Tom to the old man. "Now tell me what my dream means." "You have to promise first," demanded the dream interpreter, and Tom promised by the memory of his father. The dream interpreter was silent and looked at the cypress. The wind had died down a little, and the rustling had become a gentle whisper. Barely audible, but all the clearer, the wise man could now hear the message the wind was telling him. He listened and smiled. The words Tom had used in telling his dream were audible again. The wind had kept them and purred them into the dream interpreter's ear now. Fainter and fainter grew the wind, and soon there were but few words left. It was a quiet sentence that the dream interpreter heard before the wind stopped blowing. There was one last succession of words that echoed in his mind like a faint resound in the mountains. "I know now what your dream is trying to tell you," he said then. Tom looked expectantly at the dream interpreter.

"Be warned." The dream interpreter looked Tom deeply in the eye. "Your dream is only the beginning of a long journey. In what I am about to tell you, always remember that it is only a first step on your life's journey." Tom nodded. "Above all, don't follow the dreams of others." Tom didn't quite understand. After all, he didn't know any other dreams. "With an unfinished dream, it's easy for impatience to lead you," the old man continued. "Without being aware of it, you are so quick to follow the wrong dreams. You mistake someone else's dream for your own. And before you know it, you're living a false life. The other person's dream leads you far away from your own path in life." The old man paused. He waited because he still hoped for Tom to remember his warning, "Dreams can be deceptive. If you don't know how to interpret them, they will ruin you."

Tom had nodded repeatedly. Now it was clear to him that with this warning the old man was only trying to make Tom dependent on his interpretations. It was probably way simpler than what the old man had led Tom to believe with his mystical behavior. "So what is the message of my dream?" he asked impatiently. The dream interpreter waited a moment before answering.

"You have to think," the wise man said eventually. "That is the message of your dream." Tom did not quite understand. "What do I have to think about?" he asked, confused. "I don't know. You need to figure out yourself," said the old man. "Now go and do what your dream tells you."

Tom was disappointed and felt a bit offended. Then he got a little angry. *What kind of interpretation was that?* he thought and tried to calm down a little by thinking that at least he didn't had to pay anything for it. "I could have thought of that myself," he accused the old man. "But you didn't. After all, you're not a dream interpreter," the latter replied. With that, the old man got up and walked back to the hill from which he had come before. He had wasted enough time with this boy. He would probably never see him again, like most who buried their dreams after only a few days, even if they had known before that life had spoken to them from the very deep within. *Yet he already has everything he needs to know. He has the crystal and with it the access to the soul of the world*, the dream interpreter thought, thinking of the green emerald the boy carried with him.

When Tom returned and got into his car, he remembered what he had in his old life. *After all this nonsense, I'll just pick up where I left off before*, he thought to himself. *I knew when I got here that this time would do me no good.* Then the innkeeper had shown him a way to a nearby gas station. He hadn't asked for the dream interpreter anymore. He probably knew that most people didn't like to talk about the messages they heard from him. By now, Tom could understand that all too well.

When Tom reached the main road again, he thought of his home. He wanted nothing more than to return to his old world. Even though he knew inside that it didn't exist like that anymore. He was reminded of that by the small box that now lay on his passenger seat again.

Chapter 6

Already on the main road, Tom was thinking. What he had experienced in this short period of time wouldn't let him go. Although he was still a little annoyed with the dream interpreter, he soon realized that he was basically right. The message of the dream was so simple. Wasn't it his own fault that he had missed it? "You have to think." *Sometimes it's the simple things in life that we've forgotten to see. That's why we don't take advantage of our dreams anymore,* Tom thought, wondering about his thoughts again. "You need to think." That was the message, and suddenly he found it was the right one.

This insight improved his mood, and soon he began to look at things from a different perspective. *Wasn't there perhaps a good spell on this place? Perhaps even one that extended over the entire area?* At first, he hadn't thought anything like that when he had gone to beautiful Andalusia to get away from his life at home. But after all, wasn't there a specific reason for coming to this area in particular? Tom remembered that his father had often taken him here when he was a little boy. Some wonderful memories he associated with this country. They were also memories of his father.

Maybe I should take the opportunity to explore this area a little more after all, Tom thought. He looked over at the box on the passenger seat. *Like my father was in on it.* This time he smiled. "Where should we go?" he asked aloud, laughing a little about himself.

Tom stayed in Andalusia for three months. He had seen many places. Some of them he thought he knew from his childhood. Others were entirely new to him. But there was a magic about it all. Since he had made the decision not to return home after all, he had felt noticeably better. He had also tried to think about it further, but that had brought no new insights. *Don't push yourself to hard,* he told himself, and a saying of his father's came to his mind: *Patience brings roses.*

It was on one of his last days when he found it. The finca stood completely isolated on a small hill in the middle of a green valley. No one seemed to have lived here for years. Still, the little house made a welcoming impression. A tiny footpath led up from the gravel road to a small square, and from the short terrace there was a magnificent view over the whole area. It seemed to Tom that from up here he could see once more all the places he had travelled to in the last few weeks. Actually, he had only come up to say goodbye. But it was soon to be the real beginning of his long journey.

Tom got the idea on the road when he saw the small uninhabited house from a distance. He wanted to send a last greeting from there to the beautiful Andalusia. He wanted to take the picture of that landscape that must have presented itself from the finca home in his heart. He had consulted his little stone and was torn. At the access road, already on the property, a sign welcomed him with the clear message not to trespass on the land. Perplexed, Tom stood in front of it for a while. The finca was still a good mile or two away from there. The property had to be huge. On the other hand, the whole area looked pretty deserted. In this valley, the lots were miles apart, and he had seen the last inhabited house from the road a good half hour ago. No one would notice him. But Tom was not used to doing anything forbidden in his life. So he went back and forth whether he should enter the property despite the warning. Suddenly he found himself thinking seriously about something for the first time since the day he had met the dream interpreter and made the decision to extend his stay here. All these last months he had just let himself drift. There were no big decisions to make, no things to decide. Now, however, he was standing in front of this sign and worrying. *Could this be a sign?* So far, the decision to take one last look at the landscape from the finca had seemed pretty insignificant to him. Now it was the first thing that made him think. *Would he perhaps find another special place up there? Just as he had come to Nepanthé at the beginning of the journey? Would he take back with him something that was important to his life at home? In Nepanthé he had gained carelessness. What could he possibly gain here?* Tom remembered how he had come here over three months ago. The disorientation he had brought from home had since turned to freedom. It was freedom to travel the country without a plan or a destination. Nepanthé, the dream and its message, had changed his perspective on things. He now had the perception of a child again. This perception was focused entirely on the moment, on the beauty of nature, the singing of the birds he heard every morning, the sound of the wind and the endless landscapes. It was a glimpse of eternity. There was no past and no future. There was no time that left one disoriented. While he lingered in the moment, he once again wanted to capture all that he had experienced over the past few weeks. The place to do it, Tom felt, was this old finca on the hill in the middle of the valley.

As Tom pondered this thought and began to wonder what decision he should make, he saw a couple of butterflies. They circled the sign and then disappeared up to the finca. *Butterflies bring good luck,* his father had always said. He'd probably read it in an old book and mentioned it to Tom every chance he got since. Tom glanced at the little box beside him, then started his car and drove past the sign, following the butterflies.

The view was gigantic. Tom had not imagined it so beautiful. Earlier he had walked the grounds a little. He had discovered an old stable that must have once housed horses. An old tractor was rusting away on a path that led around the finca. From this path one could get to the old property across the meadow. Still, Tom decided he'd rather take the tiny sandy path that must have once been a small stone staircase. A few remaining ashlars that lined the path like scattered cubes still bore witness to it. Tom was glad of the decision to use the former stone stairs. That way he didn't miss the empty fountain that stood a little below the finca in a small square. There was even a swimming pool behind it, all filled in with gravel. The owner had probably not wanted to use it and therefore filled the pool with stones. The whole place provided work for a man's life. Tom remembered how, as a child, he had sunk hours into building things, fixing things, inventing things. *That is a long time ago,* he thought with a wistful smile. But it had always been an adventure, too. Suddenly, he couldn't help but think of the day he'd almost lost his hand. He had been fixing the old lawnmower. His father had let him do it, because for years every attempt to repair the machine had failed. Since then, the mower had sat unused in the old shed behind the house, rusting away. There was still some gas in the tank. Tom had squatted in front of the sharp rotor blades for hours, sticking his hand in because something seemed to be stuck. He had turned away only briefly to look for a tool, when suddenly the machine started to work. He had proudly shown the intact lawnmower to his father but hadn't said anything about the incident. Over the years, he had forgotten the story eventually. What remained, however, was his passion for anything he could build or repair with tools. In his childhood, this passion had given his heart an endless number of seemingly timeless hours.

When Tom finally stood at the top of the terrace, he knew where his dream would take him. It was written on a small white piece of paper that was still on the cottage. The finca was for sale.

Chapter 7

For a long time the dream interpreter sat by his fire and looked into the flames. The hares he had caught earlier were almost roasted. Their fat dripped into the embers and hissed. *Thoughts can confuse us,* were the first words he heard, told by the sounds the melting fat left behind. The dream interpreter bowed his head in sorrow. He had known that he would still have to help the boy. That was why it had been easy for him to delay his payment. But he hoped that the boy would make progress on his own for the time being. After all, he possessed the emerald. But what the flames told him now did not allow that conclusion.

No road is without detours, the dream interpreter thought, wondering how, with all his experience, he could keep forgetting this. He had also neglected to tell the boy about the signs. The signs that could show one the meaning of his life. That was a clear omission. He would have then also told the boy that the signs could sometimes be deceptive and that it takes a while to understand them. Especially when you had never learned to follow them before in your life. When everything was new along the way. That the boy had found Nepanthé was beginner's luck. Life always holds it in store when you set out on your journey. Beginner's luck had been needed. The boy had his stone, too, but still it could only help those who knew their heart well and could hear its voice. The boy, however, had not listened to his heart for a long time. At least not since he had grown up. *Strange*, thought the dream interpreter, *even if one has such a powerful stone as his companion, each person has first to learn again to decode the magic of the universe.*

Perhaps he should also have warned the boy more clearly about dreaming someone else's dreams. Everyone has his own dream. He certainly would have told him, had he known that the innkeeper had told the boy about his dream. The innkeeper's dream, which had destined him to build a place where there was no need to worry, was not the boy's dream. Nepanthé was right for the innkeeper. It was his dream. The boy, on the other hand, was meant to walk a path, not settle down. Not even in another place. *A change of place leads nowhere.* He had read that thought clearly in the boy's mind, after all. *Then why didn't he set out on his journey?*

Because every path has its detour, the flames crackled, and the dream interpreter was in sympathy with the deep wisdom that spoke from them. So he got up quickly after he had eaten and left the hearth, whose flames had collapsed into a cold glow by then. He had no time to lose. His haste permitted no detour.

Chapter 8

After Tom found the finca, he didn't spend much time saying goodbye to his old life. Already in Spain, he signed the purchase contract for the entire property. Tom wanted to be sure that he would be able to make his dream come true. He was afraid he would question it again once he was back home. Everyday life should not be able to touch his dream. Tom remembered well what the innkeeper had told him about the one group of people who came to Nepanthé. *They all forget their dreams as time goes by. What they are left with is a feeling that sometimes makes them wistful because once there was a dream they should have followed.* Tom would not belong to that group.

He had returned home briefly to at least take care of the most important things. In doing so, he had been able to look at his old life once again with distance. It seemed to him like a running wheel in which he had once been trapped. Tom had also observed the people around him as they went about their daily routines. *Like gears in a machine*, he thought to himself. *They have to work every day in order for the machine to function. They have no other purpose. These people are not searching for meaning in their existence. These people just function.* He wondered how they could go about their daily activities so thoughtlessly. He had once possessed this ability as well. But now it was irretrievably lost. His father's death had reminded him so painfully of the finitude of life. Then Tom thought about how life eventually ended for these people too. *They function until they are replaced.* Because even the life of a machine part is finite.

Some of his few close friends questioned his decision. Tom could see it in their looks, but hardly any of them really said anything. *They probably didn't dream for a very long time,* Tom thought and ignored their doubts.

Only his father's lawyer, who administered the estate, asked very calmly if he didn't want to take a little more time off. At least until everything was settled. He thought the purchase of the finca was rash and risky. And Tom hadn't yet put together the money for the estate he owed now. First, all his assets had to be sold so that Tom could afford his new life.

But Tom had let time go by all of his life already. At least, that was how he felt about it. Again he feared that he might be like the people of Nepanthé, who didn't cared for the meaning of their dreams. Everyday life was not to take possession of him. The longing to rebuild an old finca all by himself, forgetting the day like a child, would soon be only a distant memory. And with it, his dream.

If he was going to accept this gift that life had given him there in faraway Andalusia, then he wasn't really allowed to return home. He had sensed that over the last few months. Or had his thoughts told him that?

"A quick sale of assets is always fraught with risk," the lawyer had objected. But for Tom it was concerns that lawyers were paid to have. They always saw the risk in life. Tom wanted to see the odds at last. With the sales contract he had irrevocably committed himself to the finca. He had taken his chance. In order to pay the estate price, the lawyer would have to dispose of his assets sufficiently.

So just a few days later, he was sitting on the terrace of the finca again, watching the setting Andalusian sun. His thoughts revolved entirely around his dream. It had been over three months since he had spent that night in Nepanthé. What had come true from the dream already! His thoughts had become reality. *How far,* he wondered, *am I from the meaning of my life now?* He felt that he had taken a first right step. *The first step is always the most difficult,* Tom thought. But the Bedouin in his dream had also spoken of further tests before the purpose of his existence would be fully revealed. So it was a first step only.

Tom also thought of the dream interpreter. It had been a long time since his encounter with him. He wondered if he would find him again as easily as he had that day when he had his first dream. *Perhaps he would come to me, too. After all, dreams attract him, he had said so himself.* Then Tom remembered that the dream interpreter would still be entitled to his reward. So he would surely come of his own accord. If only to ensure that he would be paid in the end. But what might he demand? Then it flashed through Tom's mind again that it could still be his green stone that the dream interpreter would demand in the end. He felt for the box he always carried with him, and made sure it was still there. He hadn't opened it since he'd found it that time after his father's death. Now, however, he felt the need to see the stone once again. Even though the box was the same weight, he feared for a moment that the stone might no longer be inside. Someone might have switched it when he was careless for a moment. When he opened the box, however, he was relieved to find that the stone was still in place. He had never picked it up since he found the box. Perhaps the right time was now, here, on his first night at his finca, after taking an important step out of his old life. Tom was about to pick it up when he felt a small sting go into his hand and make him flinch. His finger was bleeding. Tom had forgotten how sharp the edges of the stone were. It was, after all, a shard of glass that his father had once found.

Tom bandaged his finger. The wound was deeper than he had first thought. A few drops of blood were found on the terrace. Tom was not superstitious, but he could have imagined a better sign to begin his first evening in this new life. Involuntarily he kept looking for the butterflies, but to his amazement he saw none. *Strange,* he thought, *the whole meadow was always full of them. But it's probably just too late in the evening.* He left the stone in the box and closed it again. Then he set off to go to bed.

For the first time since he had come to Spain many months ago, he felt something that he had not felt for a very long time: worry began to rise in him.

At first it was only a very slight, barely perceptible feeling that had already become completely foreign to him. His thoughts brought it to him, and Tom felt a little uneasy. Since his night in Nepanthé he had only known carelessness. Now, however, that feeling spread through Tom again as he lay in bed, brooding. *Had he, after all, perhaps been too hasty in changing his life? What had prompted him to take this step? Had he relied solely on the interpretation of a dream by an old man who claimed that the wind told him of the world soul?* Tom was startled. He would have smiled at best at such a story not so long ago back home in his old life. And hadn't the people around him done just that? Hadn't they all shaken their heads at Tom just throwing away the whole life he had back home? It wasn't a bad life, after all. It had regularities and routines, structure and stability. He didn't have to worry about anything in this life. At least with his father's inheritance, he was able to live a very independent and free life. Then he had traded all that for an almost uninhabitable finca, whose charm had consisted in the fact that he would essentially have to repair it himself. Perhaps it was the shock of his father's death that had confused him. Tom breathed heavily. He felt his heart pounding. The loud beating made him hardly rest. But then he looked at the box again and thought of his green crystal. His father's words came back to him. *The stone protects you. If it is with you, you'll be fine.* Tom got calmer again. His breathing gradually slowed. It's probably just regret after a decision that was bothering me, Tom told himself. He knew that almost all people tended to first question an important decision they had made and that it was immediately after they had implemented it.

With these thoughts, he got tired. Sleep would probably have overtaken him, as it had back in Nepanthé, if a small, stabbing pain in his finger hadn't reminded him of something. The stone that was supposed to protect him had hurt him tonight. It must have had another side, too. Tom took that last thought with him and fell asleep. And for the first time in over three months, he had a dream.

Chapter 9

"What happens when you look in the mind mirror?" Ala K'in wanted to know. The Bedouin made a serious face. "Your inside becomes your outside. The world inside becomes the world outside." *As above, so below,* Ala K'in suddenly saw it written in the ornaments of the mirror. It was the first time he had caught a glimpse of it again.

"I don't understand?" Ala K'in was a little unsettled. "You will," In Lak'ech said. "Since it has already begun." A deep, scrutinizing look from the Bedouin rested on Ala K'in before he continued, "In your search for the meaning of life, you first have to confront your thoughts. They create your reality. They can enslave you and lead you far away from the real meaning. They can distract you and lead you astray. But if you face them honestly, they will lead you a good part of the way towards your life's purpose." He looked at Ala K'in before continuing. "It is not so easy to face your thoughts. In fact, it's incredibly difficult. Depending on how you approach it, it can be one of the most difficult tasks in your entire life, perhaps even seeming unsolvable. Your thoughts become high walls of reality. Insurmountable, they lead you into a labyrinth from which you cannot find your way out if you are not careful. But see for yourself," the Bedouin spoke and pointed to the mirror.

Ala K'in couldn't help it, and let his head wander to the mirror as if entranced. The whole frame with its ornaments seemed to grow, and the words in the carvings penetrated Ala K'in's ear. *Above as below*. As his gaze crossed with the surface of the mirror, a thousand images rushed past him from the mirror. In between, Ala K'in flew and fell, losing himself completely in the world of his thoughts.

Ala K'in had fallen forever. He did not know how long or where. He had lost the orientation for where was above and where was below. Until the moment came when the falling suddenly stopped. Until Ala K'in found himself unexpectedly and somewhat surprisedly on the back of a donkey.

He noticed it by the bumpy movements. His head was lowered, and when he opened his eyes, he saw the gray-brown, shaggy fur on which was a blanket on which he was sitting. Lifting his head, his gaze traveled up the donkey's neck following the fur. He now saw the back of its head with the two ears sticking up to the sky on the left and right side. By the swaying, he realized they were moving forward. Ala K'in was actually not very comfortable with this. He couldn't ride at all, he kept thinking while searching for support with his hands. His uneasiness increased when he realized that there was only this sitting blanket he could cling to.

The sun was behind them, and Ala K'in saw his own shadow in front of him. His uncertainty about sitting on a donkey without a foothold carried over to his thoughts. It was these thoughts that also made the shadow suddenly seem large and threatening. The harder he concentrated on this impression, the more it seemed to him as if the picture the shadow drew of him and the donkey was taking on a life of its own. It was almost as if he saw in the shadow how the donkey suddenly tried to rear up and was about to throw him off. Startled, Ala K'in clung to the blanket. His finger ached, and he did not calm down until he slowly realized that he was sitting quite securely. He dared not look again at the shadow. But like a magnet, it attracted his thoughts. Fortunately, he now felt the sun on his face, and with its warming rays the thought suddenly vanished. The path had made a slight bend, and just as the sun shone in Ala K's face, the shadow disappeared sideways past them, slowly dissolving into its rays. Relieved, Ala K'in realized that he was, in fact, still sitting quietly and peacefully on his donkey.

"What am I doing here?" thought Ala K'in, noticing that he was not the only one riding a donkey. In front of him and also behind him were other men riding their animals. He was part of a group and yet he did not know how he had gotten here. Strangely, the scene seemed to remind him of something. Like an old truth he had once known, but had long since forgotten. But before he could even attempt to remember, black thoughts darkened his mind again. The leader of the donkey group seemed strange to him. Instead of exuding confidence, he struck Ala K'in as someone who would not back down from any risk. Not even if it put the group he was responsible for in danger. No sooner had Ala K'in entertained this thought than he saw the leader suddenly lead the others off the safe path they had been riding into rough terrain. Some in the group, however, seemed to take pleasure in the fact that their donkeys were swaying more and more now. They swayed and threatened to throw their owners off balance. Ala K'in felt sick with worry. He would have liked to bend forward completely flat and cling to his donkey. But he dared not. Partly out of shame, partly out of fear of possibly losing his balance for good. The leader was taking more and more reckless paths now, and suddenly the path became quite narrow. While on the right side a rock face towered, on the left it went steeply downhill. The steeper it got on this side, the faster the group leader led the donkey caravan along the abyss. Sloping down it went, and the gap seemed to get closer to the group with each step. Ala K'in already dared not even look to his left. "I have no control at all over where the man on the lead donkey is leading us," he spoke to himself. He wished fervently to no longer be a part of this group, but shortly after thinking that the next disaster loomed in front of him. The trail began to fork at the end of it. The leader turned onto the part that was flatter and safer again, and with him the donkeys that followed him immediately. The path in the other direction went around a rock and stayed on the steep track. "Please follow them, please follow them," Ala K'in thought. There were two more donkeys ahead of him to take the fork. He watched the first follow the group onto the safe path and tried to reassure himself that the second would do no differently. But Ala K'in was startled for a moment when he got the impression that the animal in front of him was about to take a wrong turn. Only when he saw that this donkey was also taking the right track did he relax somewhat. Now it was Ala Kín's turn. His burgeoning apprehension increasingly turned into panic. He couldn't shake the impression that his animal, of all things, would now bolt. His thoughts were so strongly focused on that possibility that panic turned to sheer horror when he saw that his donkey was indeed the only one taking the path around the rock. It couldn't be, it *couldn't be,* he thought as his heart began to race. But it was. The mere thought of taking the wrong direction had come true, and he was still shouting to his animal, "No, not that way, just not this way!" Ala K'in no longer knew how many no's he had inwardly shouted when the next horror loomed in front of him as well. Beyond the cliff that the donkey had been the only one headed for, the path narrowed fully into a narrow path, from which a gap now fell not only to the left but to the right as well. Ala K'in looked around for help, but all he saw was the rock he had ridden around. His companions were all gone. No one seemed to be following him. No one even seemed to have noticed that his beast had bolted from the group. Ala K'in nearly fell off his donkey when he looked back, so now he sat on his animal, cramped and almost petrified.

As if in a nightmare that wouldn't end, more thoughts flashed through Ala K'in's mind. What if it became even steeper now, if the path became narrower and narrower and in the end led into a great nothingness into which he and his animal would fall? In fact, small stones were already beginning to break away to the left and right of the path when the donkey stepped too close to the edge. The animal swayed dangerously every now and then, and Ala K'in struggled to keep his balance and not fall over with the animal. "Stop, will you," he pleaded inwardly. But the donkey marched on and on. Then he saw it. His worst fears came true. A few yards ahead of them the path ended abruptly. Behind them it went steeply downhill. They were heading for a dead end at a steep altitude from which they would not be able to get out. The path was too narrow to allow the donkey to turn back. Already every step was a possible misstep. But backwards it was utterly impossible to tread the path. The donkey could not be steered, and so Ala K'in already saw himself plunging over the cliff into the gap. He could almost feel the sensation of falling and imagined himself hitting the bottom. *This is the end,* he thought.

Chapter 10

Tom was startled when he woke up. His head was pounding. The evening's wine was causing him pain. His skull throbbed. *What kind of horrible dream had that been?* Tom had no time to think about it, for the pounding was growing louder and more unbearable. Then he realized that the pounding was coming from the door. Someone was banging loudly on the finca's door.

When he realized where he was, he got up and walked across the living room slowly to open the door. The thumping wouldn't stop at all, and Tom wasn't sure if it was his skull amplifying the banging or if there really was someone banging on the door that loud. Then it popped into his head. It had to be the dream interpreter. He hadn't really expected him so soon. But secretly Tom felt a certain satisfaction that he had not been entirely wrong the night before. *He comes for his reward. My dream has attracted him, and he is bent on interpreting it so that he can make his claim soon.* Tom was already starting to think about what the old man would tell him about the dream, which had felt more like a nightmare. When he opened the door, an answer revealed itself. Standing before him in a blush of anger was the burly, angry landowner from whom he had purchased the finca. Before Tom could say anything, he heard him roar, "Where the hell is my money?"

But there was no money left. Tom's lawyer had been right. The quick and risky sale of his fortune had attracted shady businessmen. And though the lawyer had warned him over and over again, Tom saw only the big bucks these men were offering for his property. In the end, they left, taking everything Tom owned. His fortune was gone. He owned a ruin in Andalusia, and owed the landlord full price for it. The landlord had given him a week to come up with the amount. Otherwise, he would have him thrown in jail. He knew the local judge very well, and the Spanish prisons here in the outback were not a place from which a foreigner could get out in good health. The landowner had threatened Tom, that he would be taught there that in Spain you have to keep your word.

With that, he left Tom alone at the finca. He posted a guard at the gate and Tom got his first taste of what it would feel like to be locked up. His dream had become a nightmare. Just as it was prophesied last night.

✦

Chapter 11

This week, Tom couldn't find any sleep. It was the third night in a row already. Ever since the landowner had claimed his money, Tom had been lying awake at night, unable to get any rest. He never thought his life could feel like this. So harried, so hopeless. Sometimes it felt like death. Tom was getting quiet when that feeling came.

How could all this happen? How had he been able to throw away everything he had built up over years in his old life at home? He had an proper structure that gave him security. Every day kept him busy, every night let him sleep. Tom hadn't known dreams anymore, but he hadn't known all-nighters either. He had paid for the safe routines in his life with restrictions; but didn't everyone? And what was the price he was paying now? *Too high.* Of that there was no doubt in Tom's mind. Because he had given way for a moment, been undisciplined for a moment, a dream had caused him to crash. Everything he had possessed at home was lost in one fell swoop.

If he could have, he would have bought his old life back. He would have given anything for it. Tom looked at the box beside his bed. His finger still ached. Was his green crystal, after all, possibly worth something? Tom thought of just taking it to a jeweler in the next town. Surely he could sell it there. Maybe it would at least bring in enough money to pay his way back to his old home. Since here he no longer had a future. There, perhaps, he would find his way back to his old life. From that safe ground, surely the matter of the landowner could be settled. Tom paused. Again he looked at the box. Surely there was only an old shard of glass in it. The pain in his finger reminded him of that. He was again indulging in some dream. Yet he had just learned so clearly what dreams could lead to. Dreams were dangerous.

On the fourth morning, Tom finally got up and began to fix the tractor. In the past few days, he had walked past it again and again carelessly. The tractor stood where the path that led around the finca branched off to the old shed. Tom had walked endless laps around the finca on this path over the past few days. He had racked his brains over how to get at least a little money. All his attention was focused on this question, so Tom had simply not noticed the tractor. Then he saw the butterflies. It was the first time he had seen butterflies since the day he had discovered the finca. They drew his gaze to the surroundings. Hadn't it been the sight of this landscape that had brought him here back then? He had not contemplated the beauty of this place since his first evening on the terrace. He had been so lost in the gloomy labyrinth of his thoughts that he had completely forgotten what he had come here for. Now it was the butterflies, of all things, that reminded him. Tom remembered all the things he had wanted to build and change here. This place had appealed to him because it offered so many possibilities. It was the possibilities to create something. It was the preoccupation with things that Tom had loved in his childhood. Things that he had forgotten, but that he still loved. He had come here to rediscover that love. His love of the craft. The butterflies had reminded him of that. As he looked at the tractor they were circling around, a saving idea finally came to his mind. After all, if he repaired the tractor, he could sell it later. Maybe even the landowner would accept it as a down payment. Even if that didn't work, Tom had spent his last days here doing something that had originally prompted him to buy the finca. *At least I've had a brief taste of my dream then*, he thought. He paused for a moment and looked at the old machine. *It is strange, after all, how much one is subject to the power of one's thoughts. The gloomy ones can weigh on you like lead. But when they are friendly thoughts, they sometimes give you wings.*

Tom wondered if he could learn to always think the right thoughts. He remembered his last dream and the tests that had been announced. Perhaps the first test was to find a solution to the thought problem. Maybe it was about becoming a master of his thoughts so that they no longer ruled him? As he thought about it, it seemed strange to him that one could be so at the mercy of one's thoughts as Tom had been in the past few days. *After all, my thoughts do come from me. And if the thoughts come from me, then I am their master and I can determine whether they harm or benefit me.* Tom felt that he was on the right track to pass his first test. But he also knew that the solution could not be so simple. After all, he seemed to have managed to interpret even his last dream. *I'm supposed to learn to control my thoughts.* With that realization, he felt a little better already. At least he seemed to have freed himself from the dream interpreter's dependence. *Then I can free myself from everything else,* Tom thought, now feeling a bit of confidence again. So he set about sprucing up the tractor and became completely absorbed in the moment of doing so.

✦

Chapter 12

The dream interpreter paused for a moment. He had been in such a hurry, and yet he had come too late. But now a smile slid across his face. He suddenly felt that everything was right. That it was all part of a plan that life had. The world soul hadn't told him everything by the fire. *Maybe I should have just kept listening,* he thought.

But instead of being angry about his hasty departure a few days ago, he was glad. He remembered a wise saying that had always helped him in such situations. *There lies strength in calmness.*

He had missed that in the fire that time, after the news from the flames had made him uneasy and he had left hastily. In the future, he intended to remember it. *There lies strength in calmness.* Wasn't that even written somewhere?

He intended to apply that realization right away. Secretly he was glad that he no longer had to hurry so much. Now he could walk at his natural pace again. He looked around. The sun was setting already. The dream interpreter decided to set up camp for the night and catch a few hares first.

Chapter 13

The lord of the manor sat on the terrace of his former finca and watched the boy at work. No one had ever been able to get the old tractor going, and of course the boy wouldn't be able to either. *What a dreamer! If only he'd realized that the first time he'd met him back then. Then he wouldn't have trusted him and agreed to sell the finca.* Of course, the landowner had to admit that no one had been interested in the property for years. In the end, he himself no longer expected that a possible buyer would ever contact him. He had long since stopped all efforts to sell. Only his old contact note on the window of the house still bore witness to this. In the course of time, the landowner had even forgotten that he himself had placed it there once.

He was all the more surprised when a young man contacted him a few weeks ago. At first he could hardly believe that it was about the acquisition of the old finca. Quickly he had agreed to a meeting. The story of the young man who had come into a certain inheritance and was drawn to Andalusia because of his childhood memories sounded like a stroke of luck to him. And after all this time, why shouldn't he get lucky again, he had asked himself. The interest in the finca had just been triggered by its deplorable condition. He thought the boy's plan to repair everything himself was audacious. But if necessary, he would be able to give him a hand. After all, he knew many craftsmen in the area from better times.

Now he watched this dreamer at work and thought that he should have known better. After all, he had been a dreamer himself when he had once bought the finca and all the adjoining plots in this valley many years ago. A big landowner he had wanted to be. That had been his dream. But he had stopped dreaming it a long time ago.

At first, it looked like his dream would come true. The landowner had grown up in this valley. His father was a simple shepherd, and the family didn't have much. They were happy, but as a child, he had to go without a lot. He saw the prosperity in which the children of farmers lived. He knew then that he wanted to do that one day. He worked hard and had the money for his first plot of land as a young man eventually. He knew how to farm it skillfully, and soon he had earned the money for another piece of land. With much diligence and discipline, he increased his holdings and finally was what he had always aspired to be as a child. He had made it into a wealthy landowner. But that was not enough. He dreamed of owning the whole valley where he had grown up in such poor conditions one day. The meadows where his father had once tended sheep were to be his own. On the hill in the middle of the valley he wanted to build a finca. He imagined how he would one day sit up there on the terrace and look over the whole valley.

At first, he succeeded in the plan. Just as he had previously understood how to manage the land, he also showed business acumen in acquiring the lands. It was even much easier to make money from land, he found. It also required less diligence and discipline. Prices were rising unceasingly. All one really had to do was buy the next piece of land to sell again later at a profit. The money could then be used to buy more land. And so it went on and on. In the meantime, the landowner was also able to start building his finca. An acquaintance had told him that wealth would come even faster if the banks provided the money for the land. In fact, he found that he could now acquire almost as much land in one year as he had previously earned himself in ten years. The construction of the finca was almost complete, and then came the moment when his dream collapsed.

The landowner thought back to that day, as he sat on the terrace, watching the boy working on the tractor. It was the day when a great economic crisis gripped the country. The banks demanded their money back, and the laird had to sell almost all his property far below value to pay his debts. He had lost just about everything. Apart from a last piece of land, which he now farmed himself again, all he had left was the finca. When the economy recovered a few years later, he could have sold it and used the proceeds to rebuild his business. But the crisis had not only cost him his fortune. It had also robbed him of his strength. He had aged in years. His inner fire was gone. He was resentful of himself and the mistakes he had made. He saw the loss of his property as the universe's punishment for his arrogance. Only the finca remained as a reminder of his great dream. As it decayed over the years, it also slowly caused the landowner to break. He couldn't let it go, and so it became a ruin along with him. Years later, when he did try to break away from it, it was too late. No one wanted to buy this shabby place. His dream had become a curse that he would take to his grave.

Then the boy had appeared. The landowner had believed the universe had forgiven his debt and sent this young man. With his ambition as a craftsman, perhaps he could complete what the landowner had once begun. For him, his dream would no longer be fulfilled. But he would have laid the foundation for this boy's dream. This notion filled the laird with some peace, and that was more than he had dared to hope for in his lifetime.

But the universe had tricked him maliciously because after the lord of the manor had signed over his finca to the boy, the young man's inability to pay revealed itself. It was as if fate wanted to remind the lord of the manor once again in his old age that he had not been successful in life with the sale of land.

A crash interrupted the landowner in his thoughts. He startled up from the armchair in which he had been sitting on the veranda until then, lost in his memories. Had someone fired a shot? He kept a lookout for the boy and what he saw he could hardly believe. The boy was sitting on the old tractor, driving towards the finca.

❧

Chapter 14

"Let's get something to eat." Tom was surprised to see the laird on the terrace. He had actually announced himself for the next day. He was even more surprised at his invitation. All the way down to the village they had been silent, and Tom was worried about being taken to prison after all. Maybe the invitation was just a pretext so that he wouldn't resist too much.

But Tom could be carefree because, to his amazement, the landowner actually took him to a tiny, somewhat hidden restaurant in a side street of the next village. Outside was a single, small table. It was the landowner's regular place. He often came here when he wanted to be alone to make important decisions.

The landowner ordered, and when they had eaten, he said to Tom, "No one has been able to fix this tractor yet. Everyone who has tried in the last few decades has failed. How did you manage to do it?" Tom was silent for a moment. He hesitated, but the landowner looked at him sharply. Tom still feared he would end up being locked in some cell if he didn't answer honestly. His explanation was simple, for it was that of a child. Although he feared that the landowner might dislike his answer, he finally said from the depths of his heart, "This has always been my dream."

The answer made the landowner go completely silent. A blank look was on his face. For a moment, it seemed as if his soul fell silent. Everything ceased to exist around him. There was no more feeling, no more suffering, no more joy. This nothingness that the answer had triggered in him spread to all the places he knew. The sheep pastures in the valley fell silent and on the hill of the finca the wind stopped blowing. The world stood still. And if he could have, he would have made it all end in that moment.

Tom looked at him anxiously and quickly added, "I can fix more. I was good at it when I was a kid. I can fix the whole finca if you want." Tom avoided speaking of his dream again. He also concealed from the landowner his experiences in Nepanthé and his encounter with the dream interpreter. *People react differently to strange dreams,* he thought. Tom had learned that. Back home they had ridiculed him for his dream. The innkeeper in Nepanthé, on the other hand, had helped him. He knew how important dreams were, because he had realized his own dream. He had also taught Tom that there were two groups of people. One pursued their dream, the other did not. The landowner, however, did not seem to belong to either of these groups. Tom felt that he could still learn something important here. Perhaps then he would understand why his dream had initially turned into a nightmare. Maybe Tom had ignored something. Possibly he had made a beginner's mistake. Because just as there was beginner's luck, there had to be beginner's bad luck. What if that mistake could be corrected? Could his dream come true after all? For the first time since his nightmare, Tom felt a little hopeful.

"Actually, I can fix anything," Tom said to the landowner. The latter looked at him for a long time before answering. "I don't think so," he finally said in a thin voice, then regained his composure. The landowner paused for a moment, thinking. Turning back to Tom, he said, "I'll make you a deal. If you fix up the finca, just like you did with the tractor, I'll give you enough money to go back to your home. Rebuild your life there and enjoy this second chance. You don't get them very often in life."

Tom reached under the table into his pocket for the small box. He grabbed it and thought hard about the green crystal inside. *You were right, father. The stone protects me. How could I have doubted it?* For the first time in days, Tom noticed that his hand no longer hurt. The wound on his finger had healed.

Chapter 15

Tom didn't enjoy the work as much as he thought he would. He couldn't quite put his finger on it. Perhaps because the landowner had initially had the finca transferred back to himself after Tom had accepted his proposal. True, Tom could live there until he had repaired the finca. But since he had not been able to raise the money, it was of course the landowner's property. Tom had hung the old purchase deed framed in the entrance of the house above the door. It would always remind him that he had gone the wrong way to fulfill his dream and that from now on he would solely work to be able to start all over again.

But that could not be the real reason for his lack of enjoyment at work because he still enjoyed the craft itself. Tom was also grateful to have been given this second chance through his craftsmanship. He could now even live for a while on the finca he had once wanted to buy. That was far more than he could have hoped for a short time ago. The landowner wasn't unfair, giving him a little extra pay for every bit of progress he made on the property. Thus, when all the work was completed, he would have enough money together to return to his home and resume his old life.

Perhaps it dulled Tom's enjoyment of the work somewhat that the landowner had his own ideas about how the finca should be restored. Every day he came by in the evening and not only checked the progress Tom was making, but also gave him instructions on what to do next. Nothing was good enough for him. He seemed to have an almost perfectionist idea of what the property should look like in the end.

As he lay in bed one evening, Tom remembered how he had fixed the tractor at the very beginning. That had still given him the joy he had always felt as a child. He was still completely absorbed in that work. The activity had given him peace. Peace he had needed so badly at the time, for his days and nights had been filled with anxiety and worry. He remembered the hopelessness his thoughts had led him to. The tractor had taken him away from that. So far away, that in the end, he had thought of nothing at all.

Perhaps it could also distract him from the exhausting landowner if he simply tried to immerse himself in his work. He would think less during his activity about what all this would demand of him again in the evening. And so Tom practiced immersion. Thoughts that came up he let pass. He became more and more absorbed in his work. Although the joy he had felt while repairing the tractor never fully returned, the activity gave him a little more peace. *I'm learning not to worry,* Tom noted in wonder. It was the opposite of what his dream had told him to do. *Had the dream interpreter been mistaken? He had never appeared again since their meeting then in Nepanthé. Probably he was only a charlatan after all.*

And so the weeks passed. Tom got used to the rhythm that the new life dictated to him now. The work on the finca progressed. Tom even began to feel a little pride as he watched the property slowly blossom. Only the deed over the entrance kept reminding him that it was no longer his dream he was living. *Perhaps this was part of the test the Bedouin had spoken of in his dream,* Tom thought, even if he didn't quite understand the meaning. Like he hadn't understood the first message of his dream right away, when it was just a matter of wondering. *The obvious is sometimes hard to see,* Tom thought, before he gave himself fully into the moment of his work.

One evening, when Tom had again accomplished a large section of the work, the landowner brought a bottle of wine. He was not a bad man, not only fair but generous. Tom wondered, why he was so very different when it came to the finca.

They sat together on the terrace and looked into the dusk. Silently they enjoyed the wine. The landscape reminded Tom of the first time he had come here. Back then he had aimlessly explored his life and this area, and once again he felt something of the freedom he had felt back at that time.

After they had sat side by side like this for a while and the wine was running low, Tom took heart and asked the estate owner about the finca. Until then, Tom had not dared to talk about anything but work. He sensed that it was something very personal that connected the landowner to the finca. The memory of his reaction back then in the small restaurant was still present in Tom's mind.

"Why is the finca so important to you?" he finally asked, after the wine had helped him a little to gather all his courage. The landowner hadn't expected the question. But he looked quite differently this time. His gaze still fixed on the landscape, a slight smile brushed his face. "Because it was once my dream," he spoke towards the valley. Then he told Tom his story. How he had worked his way up from a poor little family of sheepherders to a great landowner, and how he had lost it all again before he could enjoy his success up here. He released his heart from a burden he had been carrying around since those days. Never before had he talked to anyone about it. But this boy was a stranger in the valley. He had appeared out of nowhere and with him the old finca had returned to the landowner's life. The boy had reminded him of an old truth that his silence had tried to cover all these decades, but that he could not forget. The truth that his dream had been shattered. It was the realization that he was one of the people who pursued their dreams but in the end, couldn't muster the strength to make them a reality. It was the people who faced one last great test, which was to find out if they really wanted to fulfill their dream, and who failed in that test. Just as the landowner had not wanted to start all over again when the opportunity presented itself and when he'd held on to the finca instead. Just like when he couldn't let go of the past and therefore dragged a millstone through his life that left him old and tired.

"But then your dream is just coming true," Tom said. He was quite cheerful, and pointed to the finca, which had already begun to bloom again in so many places. Seriously and a little wearily, the landowner turned to Tom. "No, my son, you are fulfilling that dream. This is something entirely different." Tom thought of how the dream interpreter on the mountain had told him that one should not pursue another's dream. Then he wondered if he already knew what his real dream was. "Dreams are deceptive. They deceive us, just as we can deceive ourselves all our lives," the landowner continued. "My dream showed me that it was only pride that guided me all these years. I wanted to own the sheep meadows where my father grazed his flock. I wanted to be above all those I had envied for their prosperity as a child. But in the end, life showed me that was an aberration." Tom looked thoughtfully at the old man. Was he, too, on a wrong track? Hadn't it been the nostalgic childhood memories in the face of his father's death that had made him give up his life and come here? Or was it perhaps only a detour? Tom felt that he was still at the beginning of his journey. He was not yet as old and tired as the landowner. Tom still had the strength and the will to make his dreams come true in life.

After looking at the landowner for a while, he finally asked, "But then what is your dream?" Calmly, with a glance that was done with life, the landowner looked Tom in the eye. "I never really tried to find out." After that, they were both silent for a long time.

The wine was finished and the landowner got up. Tom thanked him for the evening, and as they were about to say goodbye, it occurred to Tom that the landowner hadn't even properly answered his first question. "But if the finca isn't your true dream at all, why is it still so important to you?" he asked. The landowner looked at the boy intently before answering, "It's like any false dream you pursue in life. In the end, it's harder to let it go than to continue living with it unfulfilled. The finca keeps me alive. It sustains the last of my life force, and in return I give it the hope of blossoming again someday. As I need it to live, over time it needs me." And as he walked, he added, "Besides, it gives me a little pleasure to see her evolve. Just as it gives you pleasure to be completely absorbed in the moment of your work."

That evening Tom took the framed deed off the wall. He would not tie his life to a false dream. He felt that he would soon set out and continue his journey.

Chapter 16

Tom was already in his bed and about to fall asleep when there was another knock at the door. The landowner had probably not even made it all the way to the main road and then abruptly turned back. It must have been another important thought that had occurred to him as he was leaving the estate, if he had once more got Tom out of bed so late.

Tom remembered the morning many months ago when he had come up from his nightmare and the pounding on the door had given him a headache. How glad he was that this knocking now sounded quite polite and downright quiet, quite as if he were not to be roused from his sleep this time. So Tom walked through the prepared living room to the front door, thinking how different people could be. There he had been not so long ago with an angry, incensed laird who had nearly kicked his door in, and now it was a very different person who was knocking. This person was circumspect and downright reserved, probably because he was afraid of waking Tom up.

But when he opened the door, Tom realized he was mistaken. It was not the landowner at all who knocked. Tom could hardly believe his eyes. Before him stood the dream interpreter. He greeted Tom with a cheerful smile. "Won't you invite me in? Surely you have been waiting for me for some time?" spoke the wise old man, and stepped into the entrance hall. "Nice house you've found here," he said, as he was about to go into the living room and make himself comfortable in one of the plain upholstered chairs. "I'll have some tea, if you don't mind," said the old man immediately after he had taken his seat. Tom was speechless. But since he was awake now anyway, he decided to make the old man's tea and then join him. The fireplace was burning already when he returned from the kitchen with the tray. Tom was puzzled. He was sure he hadn't even fixed the fireplace yet.

Tom handed the old man the tea and sat down with him in silence. After they had sat like that for a while, the dream interpreter spoke, "You have passed your first test. You just don't seem to be aware of it yet." Tom was puzzled again. This time he hadn't even told the dream interpreter anything about his second dream. "I don't think the thoughts I've been having have made me pass a test," Tom objected. He was doubting again the abilities of this old codger. The old man had probably had all the trouble in the world to locate Tom at all and was certainly only after his reward. Probably they had long since realized in Nepanthé that he was a quack and had chased him away. Now he was probably looking for old contacts and trying to get his payment. For a moment it occurred to Tom that perhaps the dream interpreter was part of a larger gang. He'd be able to handle the old man, after all. But what if he had brought men with him, waiting outside? *Probably he just wants to scout around to see if I have any money up here, and then have me mugged. Or maybe he still cares about my crystal.* Tom realized, a little startled, that he had forgotten the box next to his bed when he had just gotten up. Maybe the old man was just here to distract him while someone got into the house in the back and robbed the crystal.

The dream interpreter had followed Tom in his thoughts and smiled mildly before speaking. "You didn't actually pass a test with your thoughts. They just led you into a nightmare." Tom had just been looking for an excuse to go back to the bedroom and get his box, when he paused immediately. The dream interpreter watched, somewhat amused, as Tom pondered how the old man could possibly know about his nightmare. Before Tom's thoughts could lead him further astray, the dream interpreter continued, "Just as your thoughts often terrify you, they have led you into a nightmare. You should really notice how much they always trouble you in your life. Just as they make you fear at this moment that your beloved heartstone is being stolen." Tom stared at the old man. Had he really just been able to read his mind? Tom felt a little ashamed. "It's all right," said the wise man, "I'm used to perceiving worse thoughts. Over time, you learn to deal with it when you experience things that aren't meant for you. That's the price I have to pay for this gift." Tom didn't quite know what to say to that. He still felt a little ashamed. But as he thought about it, it struck him how often he had accused the old man of bad intentions.

"I've come for my reward, of course," the old man said mischievously. "But before that, you have two more trials to pass. That is why I have to interpret your last dream for you. Only then can you continue your journey. That is what I am here for." Tom realized that the old man was right. True, Tom had succeeded in immersing himself more and more in his work at the finca, and in shutting off his thoughts. But there was one thing he had been thinking about many times lately: What was it about his nightmare? Why did he think he was following his dream at first, only to find himself on a wrong track? "It's a detour," the dream interpreter said. "Just as I have often had to take detours in my life to get where I want to go," he added mildly. Tom looked at him. "Is that why you took so long to find me?" There was something accusing in Tom's voice. For a moment he thought back to the morning after his nightmare when he had gotten up and expected to find the dream interpreter at his door. It certainly would have saved Tom a lot of grief if he had come to him back then and interpreted his dream. "You needed the time, so I was not allowed to come sooner," said the old man wisely. Tom looked at him skeptically. *The old man knows how to turn a word in one's mouth,* he thought, and immediately wished he had thought better of it. Tom could tell by the old man's smile that he had been able to read that thought, too.

"Then we're still in business?" the old man asked searchingly. "Yes, we are still in business." Tom acknowledged their agreement that at the end of his journey he has to give the dream interpreter whatever the latter demanded. *I must not think of my stone,* he thought at the same time. But the worry that the dream interpreter would continue to read his mind was unfounded since he was already asking Tom to look into the flames of the fireplace.

"What do you see?" the dream interpreter asked. Tom thought for a moment, then said the first thing that came to his mind, "Everything's on fire." The old man grinned. "You see, my boy, that is the answer your thoughts bring to you. But now look once again into the fire. Look at the fireplace as if you yourself had restored it. Then tell me again what you see." Tom was puzzled for a moment. He tried to remember, and with the search of that memory a picture revealed itself. He suddenly saw himself sitting by the fireplace, repairing it. In his mind he finally lit the fireplace and looked into it. It was at the sight of the flames that he felt it, and as if in a trance he now answered the dream interpreter: "I feel the moment. I see the great nothingness of eternity. I feel quiet joy and the peace that this moment brings me." The dream interpreter nodded in satisfaction. "Just as you have felt that peace in everything else you have done here at the Finca," the old man said.

It was then that Tom understood that it was this fulfilling moment from his childhood that he had been searching for and found here. He understood that it wasn't his destiny to live on a finca in Spain, but that he had to learn to capture such a moment again on the way to finding his purpose in life. Just as he had known no time as a child, he needed to be able to lose himself in the moment as an adult if he was to make any progress on his quest. Perhaps the moments in which he lost himself timelessly were something like breadcrumbs that could lead him out of a dark forest that his life had sometimes felt like.

The old man was pleased with what he saw. "As I said, you have passed your first test." He poured the rest of the tea into the fireplace, putting out the fire. "Now go to sleep. Your next dream will confirm what I have said. Your second test already awaits you."

The dream interpreter remained sitting by the extinguished fire for a while and listened to the whispering of the fireplace. As Tom lay in bed, growing weary, he had to think again of his nightmare. At the point where his thoughts had almost made him fall into an abyss, he fell asleep.

Chapter 17

"Only one more step," thought Ala K'in, "only one more step, and we will crash." He saw the gap again towards which his donkey went. Only a few meters separated him from the abyss.

Only one more step. At that thought, a memory arose in him. He thought and suddenly felt that there was something he had just learned after all. Slowly, and like a slight puff of air, the memory came back to Ala K'in. It was all about the moment. Only the moment mattered. Ala K'in's mind raced. But his heart turned calm. He suddenly realized that this moment was all there was. Everything else was meaningless. Someone had taught him that, he thought. As he got more and more aware that neither the wrong turn down the path and his looking back, nor the precipice at the end of the path and his impending fall were real at this moment, he got calmer. They were only thoughts that tried to bring the past back to life or foresee the future. Then, Ala K'in reflected on an old truth. Peace returned to him and something within him sensed that he was sitting on a beast that he had once felt love for. He didn't know where this feeling came from, but he knew that this one moment was all that mattered. The moment in the here and now, sitting on his donkey that had carried him safely through all adversity so far. He felt the blanket and the animal. Heart warmth rose within him and without any further notice, gap and abyss and fear and terror disappeared. In that one perfect moment, it seemed to Ala K'in as if he watched himself sitting calmly and happily on the donkey. But to his amazement, it was the image of a little boy he saw, and when he looked more closely he realized that it was a mirror that reflected the boy on a donkey. Gradually, however, the image dissolved and Ala K'in found himself again in the desert.

"You have learned your lesson," In Lak'ech smiled at him. Perplexed, Ala K'in sat at the table with the mirror and looked in wonder at the Bedouin. And as if anticipating the question of what it all meant, In Lak'ech looked at him and said, "I will explain everything."

Chapter 18

The dream interpreter was still sitting in front of the fireplace, listening to the crackling sound of the long extinguished fire. The sounds came from the fireplace like echoes of the past. Hardly anyone would have been able to notice them. But the dream interpreter knew the language of the flames, even when they were silent.

He once again thought about the conversation he just had with the boy. But in the silence of the ashes, it was the Bedouin who now spoke to his protege. He also explained that it was the moment when someone found peace from his thoughts. Immersion in the moment could offer protection. *Like a weapon, a cloak of protection, or a spell that kept one from evil.*

Satisfied, the dream interpreter looked into the dust of the fireplace. He felt as if he could see the desert in it, where everything Tom had described to him had taken place. Now he had learned his first lesson. The immersion had freed him from his bad thoughts. Realizing that everything except being in the here and now was an illusion had saved him from falling into the abyss and perhaps even from death.

The dream interpreter could hear Tom tossing and turning in his bed next door. His second test would certainly not be as easy as the first.

✦

Chapter 19

"Trust in the moment. It's the only thing that's real. If it feels right, you're on the right path and everything will be fine. Your thoughts are an illusion. They create something that is long gone or show you a future that doesn't exist yet. Dwell in the moment if you want to make progress in your search for the meaning of life." With that, the Bedouin concluded his explanations. Now Ala K'in understood how he had escaped the gorge of death and ruin, and what had brought him from his perilous experiences in the mind-mirror back to the desert and to In Lak'ech.

Ala K'in had a universal insight. But he also sensed that it could not yet be the final answer to the question that had brought him here. "Even if I am aware of the moment, how do I find the meaning of life?" he asked the Bedouin doubtfully. "Well," said the Bedouin gently, "that is part of your second test."

Ala K'in still had so many questions. But when he looked up again, he realized that In Lak'ech had disappeared. Where just a moment ago the Bedouin had been sitting in front of the mirror, the only thing that now was left was the palm tree that provided a little shade. "In Lak'ech," shouted Ala K'in into the vastness of the desert, "where are you? What am I supposed to do? What is my second task?" But there was no answer.

Desperate and alone, Ala K'in sat in the palm tree's shadow and stared into the desert. A moment ago he had learned an important life lesson: that one should live in the moment and not focus too much on the future or the past. It was the first step to finding the meaning he was looking for in his life. But now he was unsure. Should he just sit here and dwell in the moment? Was this the second test? Ala K'in felt it was not about that. Hadn't In Lak'ech also taught him that one should listen to that inner voice, no matter what it was saying?

"But then what?" he thought to himself. "Am I supposed to look for a way out? Is that the task you set for someone you leave alone in the desert?" Ala K'in was clueless. He tried to concentrate. He listened to see if he could hear his inner voice, but he heard nothing. For quite a while he sat like this under the palm tree, pondering, until he got hungry and thirsty and remembered that he had nothing to eat or drink. *I won't survive a single night here,* he thought. But then he paused. No, he wouldn't let his thoughts take control of his life again. It took him a tremendous effort, but with all his mental strength he managed it. He accepted the starving. He accepted the thirst. When a thought came up that showed him a worrisome future, he paused and tried to stay in the here and now and to immerse in the moment. So Ala K'in sat there under the palm tree in the desert, not even noticing how fatigue overcame him. In the shade of the palm tree, he peacefully fell asleep.

"We need to leave soon," was the first thing he heard. It sounded like a voice in a dream, but when he heard it for the second time, he opened his eyes and was surprised. He glanced around and looked in the direction from which the voice might have come, but for miles there was no one in sight. "We need to leave soon." He heard it again. Ala K'in looked up and saw that there was something. But could the voice have come from what was directly facing him?

In front of him stood his donkey, looking at him faithfully. "Where did you come from?" asked Ala K'in, as he could see no tracks in the sand. But he forgot the question right away when he saw that the donkey was carrying supplies and water. Sighting this, Ala K'in's hunger and thirst came back into his mind. He grabbed the supplies and first had some water.

"We need to leave soon," he suddenly heard the voice say again. In shock, he almost dropped the water. He turned around, but there was no one. Nor was anyone to be seen anywhere. He slowly turned back to his donkey and looked at the animal. "Will you come now?" he heard the voice again. He looked deeply into the donkey's eyes. Ala K'in could detect nothing special in the look, and yet he wondered if it was the donkey talking to him. "Where do we have to go?" asked Ala K'in.

There was no reply. He was probably wrong. *Nevertheless, the question is where I should set out*, Ala K'in thought. *Now that I have a donkey and some supplies, perhaps I should ride off into the desert. I might find something there that I should be looking for. Even if I don't know what it is. After all, it can't be the point of this test to lie around here under the palm tree.* With that, Ala K'in swung onto his donkey and rode off.

"Finally, here we go." He heard the voice and winced a little. This time he didn't even try to look around. Ala K'in watched his donkey for a while, wondering whose head that voice was really coming from. Was it the donkey's, or in the end, his own? "Where shall we ride to?" The voice interrupted his thoughts. Ala K'in decided it was the donkey talking to him, even if it didn't give the slightest appearance of doing so. *Better than talking to myself,* Ala K'in thought. *My donkey will talk to me, then.*

Ala K'in thought about which direction he should take from now on. *You decide where we go,* he thought looking at his donkey. Then he swung the reins, and the animal started to move.

So they rode into the endless desert. Ala K'in did not know what he was actually looking for and which direction he should take. He let his donkey decide and rode with him for what felt like an eternity through the sand under a sun that seemed strangely mild and pleasant. "It is getting dark," he suddenly heard the voice say. Ala K'in hadn't even noticed that the sun was no longer high up in the sky but slowly setting. "Before the sun sets, we have to make camp for the night," the voice said, and Ala K'in, turning to his donkey, replied, "You are right." "Have we reached our destination?" the voice asked back. Ala K'in did not know. He didn't know at all what he was looking for here, or if there was anything to find. The Bedouin had disappeared and just the donkey and a strange voice were left. "What are we looking for?" Ala K'in asked the donkey silently, not knowing any better. "Perhaps you can tell me what we should be looking for?" he kept asking. It took a while. Silence reigned. Was the donkey thinking? Ala K'in was pondering whether the animal might actually be thinking when he heard the voice again, "If you don't know, how can I?"

Disheartened to find no real answer this way, he brought his animal to a halt. *Alright, let's make camp for the night,* Ala K'in thought and prepared everything. The sun was already setting and he could feel the desert, which had been warm and pleasant just a moment ago, slowly getting cold. After he had shared some of the remaining supplies with his donkey and after the sun had slowly disappeared from the horizon, he lit a fire. *What are we looking for?* he wondered again. About a hundred times Ala K'in thought about that, then great tiredness overcame him and with nightfall, he had finally fallen asleep.

When he awoke the next morning, he saw the bright sun in the sky first. It was almost noon already, but it was still pleasantly cool on the spot where he lay. Ala K'in was just beginning to wonder about this when he realized that he was no longer lying on the spot where the fire had still burned during the night. Startled, he straightened up and found his donkey gone as well. He tried to control his rising panic, as he had learned to do, when he discovered a shadow on the ground. It was probably the reason the spot he had been lying on was so pleasantly cool. When Ala K'in turned around to find the long shadow's source, he was surprised to see the palm tree, from which he had set out yesterday, in front of him.

But before he could even think about whether it was really the same palm tree, he heard the voice speak again, "We need to leave soon." When he turned around again, he saw his donkey. But something was different. He looked at the supply and the water bag. They were packed as they had been the day before. "Let's get going," he heard the voice say.

So, a new attempt. Well, some strange things have happened to me here, he thought. It *had probably been the wrong way yesterday.* He swung on his donkey, pulled on the reins, and steered the animal in the opposite direction from the day before. "I'll decide this time," he said to his animal, and was surprised to find that the voice answered, "If you know where you're going ..."

So they went a second time and a third, and over and over again Ala K'in found himself under the palm tree the next morning. No matter in which direction he rode, no matter where he camped at night, no matter who made the decision as to where to ride: Each time, all paths led him back to the palm tree from which he had ridden out that first morning. Ala K'in felt as if he were discovering eternity. It seemed to him that not only days and months, but years and decades had passed that he had spent like this. There were times when he felt like he had become an old man. Even his donkey was getting on in years, dragging itself with difficulty through the hot desert sands. At other times he felt young and fresh again, like a young adult traveling with a strong and young animal. For a while, these conditions seemed strange and unnatural, but then he remembered the Bedouin saying that time and space did not exist in this world.

Ala K'in almost no longer remembered the Bedouin's name, that long ago seemed their encounter. It had taken place so many days ago until the Bedouin had said something and then disappeared. What was it after all? What had the Bedouin told him? Ala K'in couldn't remember when a voice he couldn't quite tell if it was his own, someone else's, or his donkey's repeated the Bedouin's last sentence, "This is part of the second test."

What, Ala K'in thought at that moment, *what was part of the second test? What had the Bedouin said he was supposed to learn here?* It took him almost forever to remember, but when he woke up the next morning in his palm tree's shade and saw his donkey, he knew what he had to do.

Chapter 20

Rays of sunlight woke Tom up. They slowly broke through the window shutters and let some light into the dark bedroom. It was already a little later in the morning, for Tom had slept longer than usual. The first thing he realized was that he had been dreaming again. Just as the dream interpreter had predicted. This time it seemed like an interminably long dream to Tom and he wondered if he had been lying here in his bed forever. Years seemed to have passed since the dream interpreter had reappeared and had been having tea with him by the fire.

When he went into the living room somewhat dazed, there was indeed no dream interpreter sitting there any longer. But then Tom saw the ashes of the night before in the fireplace. It must have been his dream that had given him that feeling of eternity. Slowly he remembered that he had crossed the desert an infinite number of times. He had been searching for something he couldn't find, and every morning he had set out once more from the same spot. Just when he knew what he had to do, he had woken up. As much as he tried, Tom couldn't remember how to pass this test.

He made himself some coffee to revive, for he still felt as if he had slept for half a century. Everything looked as it always did outside, and only the missing deed over the front door reminded him of the conversation with the landowner the night before. Tom would not chase a false dream like the landowner did. He had remembered that. *But what is my true dream?* He remembered the Bedouin's words. *Trust in the moment. It is the only thing that's real. If it feels right, you're on the right path.* In his dream, that realization had felt so perfectly right. But now, Tom almost didn't know anything to do with it.

He looked at his watch and noticed that it was almost noon. If he didn't start his work soon, he wouldn't be able to present any progress to the landowner tonight. So he decided to stop thinking about his dream and turned to his work. Today he wanted to repair the old fountain, and that would be a good bit of work. Eventually, perhaps, the dream interpreter would reappear and help him interpret his dream. But even if that won't happen, Tom suddenly felt an inner serenity to just let things come to him. *My life hasn't felt like this since that time I was in Nepanthé,* Tom thought satisfied. He thought of his green crystal, still in the box beside his bed. For the first time, he didn't carry it. Up here at the finca, he didn't have to worry about losing it. Thinking about that, he noticed that something had changed in him. While he had always been tormented by thoughts of loss or worry, he now felt some serenity. The dream interpreter had shown him that his thoughts often terrified him. The very fear of losing his stone was unjustified all the time and had created much distrust in him. Now, however, he was perfectly calm and composed regarding this thought. *You have passed the first test.* Tom remembered the dream interpreter's words.

With this in mind, he set to work and became completely absorbed in his activity. He was eager to see where the second test would lead him. With the joyful certainty that he had followed his path so well so far, he looked forward to the events that were yet to come. Had he known what awaited him, he would have quit his quest for sure.

Chapter 21

Eleven months and nineteen days had passed since Tom had repaired the tractor. In the meantime, the finca had fully awakened to a new life.

Tom had rebuilt the old stable, which now gave shelter to horses again. One of the landowner's farmhands now regularly drove his tractor over the fields and farmed the land. The main path around the estate had been rebuilt. Magnificent hedges fenced in the hill on which the finca was situated, and flowers and almond trees bloomed in the meadow. The little path leading up to the house had been expertly repaired by Tom. A small staircase of granite stones now led along the picturesque path to the beautiful veranda and passed the splashing fountain in the little square. Behind it, Tom had cleared the pool of gravel and in the clear, fresh water one could now swim towards the horizon. The place was perfect.

When the landowner came that evening Tom was sitting on the terrace counting his money. He had now earned enough to return to his old home and resume his old life. When the landowner saw Tom like this, his heart ached a little. He had gotten used to the boy during these past months. The evening visits had become a regular ritual, and while in the beginning, he had mostly wanted to check on the work and keep track of progress, he had to admit that it was now the conversations with this boy that had given him more than he could have ever hoped for. He could hardly imagine what it would be like up here without the boy.

"What about your dream?" the landowner asked as they sat on the terrace enjoying some wine.

Tom looked at the landowner thoughtfully for a while. "I'm still figuring it out," he finally said. "I thought this finca was my lifelong dream. Rebuilding it the way I wanted to rebuild my life felt right. But then I realized it was merely a memory of the past that fooled me. The thought of being able to feel the ease of childhood again led me astray. I had thought that I could resurrect the memories I had of my father, with whom I often came to this country as a young boy. But time cannot be brought back. It is irretrievably gone. If you focus your thoughts too much on the past, they will inevitably take over. The same is true for the future. That's what I've learned here." Tom paused before continuing.

"I have learned to immerse myself in my day's work. I've melted into the countless moments that have occurred over the past few months. They have connected me to everything I have done. That's how I've been a tractor and a fountain. I've felt the old barn come to life again, and felt the joy of the craggy staircase that you can now climb back up to this place. My soul has been touched by all of this countless times.

Now I feel a deep connection. The finca has become a part of me, and I am a part of it."

The landowner listened to the boy's words. A tear ran down his face. The boy had come closer to this place as he had ever been able to. It made the landowner proud and sad at the same time. This place had a soul now. But it was not his. He reflected on the boy's words and felt joy rising. Life had returned to this place. He too was connected to the finca, though in a different way. Just as the boy had made things come alive again, the landowner now felt life within again that he had thought lost for so long.

"The finca was not my dream," the boy continued. "I learned that it was immersion that I was to experience here. This place was just the first test I had to pass. It was to show me that thoughts and false dreams can lead to the abyss and that the pursuit of one's life's dream encompasses the ability to experience the moment in its full beauty." Tom looked at the landowner. "That is the gift I have found here, and for which I am grateful to you as well."

Satisfied, the landowner looked at him. He realized that he had accomplished far more than just having his old finca rebuilt, and that filled him with peace. "How will you find your life's dream now?" he asked the boy after he had gazed for a while at the setting sun on the horizon.

"I don't know," said the boy. "In the dream, I already knew. There I wandered to find that destination. Endlessly I searched for it, not knowing what it was. A voice made me start over and over again. Restlessness spread through me, and so, as I ask myself every day what is the meaning of my existence, I have crossed the desert for an answer." "Where has your search led you?" asked the landowner. He made himself aware that he himself had never sincerely tried to sense his true meaning in life, and felt that he could still learn something from this boy.

"My search kept setting me back. Every day I began anew in the same place. No matter what I did, I never reached my destination. Whatever I did, the desert made me start my journey all over again. But I already have the knowledge within me. Because I had it in my dream. I believe it is my second test to make myself aware of this realization in order to get closer to my life's dream." Saying these words, Tom thought of his green crystal. *He already knows where your path will take you. It will lead you.* Those were the words of the dream interpreter, and Tom realized how right he was after all about everything.

"Where do you want to go now?" the landowner asked him. He glanced at the money Tom had been counting all day and still held in his hands. "You have earned enough to return to your old home." Tom looked at the money and thought for a while. He touched the little box that he had in his pocket and finally said, "Not so long ago I had believed that I could return to my old life. I wanted to forget what happened to me here when I lost the finca and all my possessions." Tom looked at the landowner gratefully. "Now, however, I do not want to miss what has been given to me as a gift here as a result. Just as I could not resurrect the memory of my childhood, so I cannot go back to my old life, which after all no longer exists in that way. I no longer have a home. But all paths are open to me now. I may not know my destination, but I will go where life sends me to reach it."

The landowner looked at Tom for a long time. There was something comforting in the deep serenity that spoke from the boy. Again he felt the desire to have the boy around. "Let's celebrate a little the rebuilding of the finca tomorrow," he suggested suddenly. "Take the day off. You've almost never left this place. Explore the village and the area. When you return in the evening, I will have dinner prepared. Then we'll see where your path takes you next." Tom accepted the offer gratefully, wondering if there was anything else the landowner intended by this invitation.

❧

Chapter 22

The girl stood at the top of the stairs that led to the finca. Her beautiful face reflected the evening sun. She smiled. Tom was very excited as he climbed the stairs to the finca. He had never seen a girl like her. She looked like an angel. As the smile turned into a radiant laugh, a feeling took hold of him that Tom had been completely unaware of until now. He felt love. When he had climbed the last step to the finca and stood in front of the girl, he was transformed. There was a magic in his life now that he had not known since his childhood days. Everything felt light and carefree. He didn't need to be absorbed in his work to know that this moment was perfect. And from now on, every moment in his life would carry that perfection. Tom had arrived.

He remembered his childhood's magic. He thought of his father and the ease that life had back then. Now he felt that ease too, but there was more. Tom was floating. Looking at the girl, he felt a deep connection like he had never felt in his life before, not even to his father. Tom felt the world soul. His green crystal, which was in the open box beside his bed as it always did, was part of the *Tabula Smaragdina* indeed.

It revealed the secret that the world soul held. Tom just had to look at the girl and could feel how everything was connected. It was enough to be in her presence to see life in all its perfection. *Everything is right the way it is,* Tom thought, filled with love. His stone had led him here. His father's death had not been in vain. It had shown him the way to this enchanting being and to the meaning of his existence.

"You must be Tom," the girl said. Tom, who until then had thought he already knew love at the sight of it, now experienced what perfection felt like when he heard the sound of her voice. Had Tom already heard that voice in his dream? He was not sure. Was she the inspiration he had dreamed of while still in the desert, just before he woke up? He was almost certain. But what he really knew for sure was that life without this girl was henceforth unthinkable.

"I am Juanita," said the girl, and with each of these words Tom felt enchanted. He must have stood there as if in a trance, because the girl smiled sheepishly and told him that the landowner was cooking inside already. He had invited her because he was eager to introduce her to the young man who had turned this old ruin into a living estate again. "You must know magic," she said with the gratitude of a little girl getting back something long lost. Her gaze rested on Tom, but he was still unable to say anything. *This must be what a dream feels like,* he thought.

The landowner appeared and interrupted the harmonious silence in which the two stood looking at each other. "You have already met, how nice," he said briefly. "I hope you are not angry with me for bringing company with us on our last evening." Tom could not imagine how he could have been angry with the landowner. But his words reminded him that he would soon be leaving this place. This thought hurt. He envied the landowner for the young girl who cared for him.

As it turned out, Juanita had nursed the landowner in his sick days. "If it hadn't been for Juanita, I'm sure I wouldn't be alive," the landowner told over dinner. He smiled, and Tom wondered what kind of love it was that tied the landowner to the young girl. It seemed to be a different love from the one he felt. But perhaps that was due to his age.

They had talked for a long time during dinner. Tom had never talked so much since he had arrived here many months ago. The landowner watched the way the girl looked at Tom. He saw something in her look that he had never seen before. He sensed it was a love far beyond what she had always felt for him. When the time came to say goodbye to each other, the landowner took Tom aside. "Where will you go now?" he asked him searchingly. "I don't know," replied Tom, trying to cover the slight despair which the thought of parting caused in him. "I think I will go to my old home first, and then think it over." The landowner looked at him for a while. "I think it will be better if you think about it here," he said then. After these words, he turned to the girl who had already been waiting for them at the stairs. "Tomorrow, my darling, Tom would like to show you the tractor he fixed." He gave her a kiss on the cheek. "I won't be able to be there, but I'm sure he'll take good care of you." With a smile, he turned back to Tom. "Take good care of my daughter. She's a gem. And a gem is a rare thing to find in life." Tom looked at the landowner. Now he knew that he would spend the rest of his life on this finca.

Chapter 23

Another five months and sixteen days had passed since his first encounter with Juanita when Tom drove to the village to run errands. Life seemed to have gone by in a flash. As he strolled through the small streets, he thought back to the moment he had confessed his love to the girl. She had wanted to see the tractor her father had told her about at the very beginning. Tom had encouraged her to climb up on the seat with him, although she had been a little worried because the machine was so big and heavy. "Everything will be fine when I'm with you," Tom had said, and she had smiled. They had been driving for a while across the fields of the valley when Tom stopped at an almond tree. Still sitting on the tractor, he had told her how much he loved her. His heart was beating faster, but at her first smile already he saw that she felt the same way. They had found each other. If butterflies had been flying around her, Tom would have proposed right away. Now he was glad that moment was yet to come. *We have all the time in the world,* he thought, wondering when he would ask her.

Tom suddenly realized that he was standing in front of the small restaurant where the landowner had offered him to repair the finca back then. *Was it a sign? Should he ask her father for her hand first, as it was the tradition?* Tom wondered. He knew by now that Juanita's father always came here when important decisions had to be made. As he approached the diner with the small table in front, he noticed an old man sitting in the landowner's regular seat. He wouldn't have noticed him if he hadn't been sitting at that table. In all the months he had lived here, he had never seen anyone but the landowner sitting there. But as he walked up to the old man, he noticed who was sitting right there in front of him.

"I've always been with you. You just never noticed me," the dream interpreter greeted him somewhat wistfully. Tom wondered. He had believed that the old man had disappeared forever after that night by the fireplace. He already worried that something might have happened to him since his disappearance had come so suddenly and without a goodbye. However, having heard of no accidents in the area, Tom reassured himself that the dream interpreter had probably just been in need of money and would seek out other contacts around the country to collect outstanding payments. He felt sorry for the old man. "Can I join you?" asked Tom, sitting down with the old man to keep him a little company as well without waiting for an answer. Delighted, he told the dream interpreter of his experiences. He told of the completion of the finca and of his friendship with the landowner. He told of how the latter had invited him to dinner at the finca the previous evening and how that evening had changed his life. When he spoke of the girl, the dream interpreter looked at him quietly. *He probably wants to know about my last dream,* Tom thought, wondering why the wise man didn't seem to read his mind. *Perhaps he is too old by now and is gradually losing his special gift,* Tom thought sadly. If it had been distrust with which he had met the old man last time, he now felt pity for him. Tom decided to tell him about his last dream. It might cheer him up. He told about the Bedouin and that he had indeed passed the first test, as the dream interpreter had predicted, because he had stopped worrying. He explained how he had learned to immerse himself in the moment. He reported that he had ridden aimlessly on his donkey through the desert countless times and had finally come to another realization that last morning under the palm tree.

"I know now what I already knew at the end of my last dream in the desert." Tom looked at the dream interpreter, beaming with joy. He was so euphoric that he didn't notice how the old man grew quieter and almost seemed a little sad. "There is no destination. Life doesn't work that way. One believes one needs to seek out goals, just as I set out over and over again in the desert in my dreams. It is a voice that the universe sets within us. Some don't hear this voice at first. But those who have learned to be completely with themselves and rediscover their inner voice, hear in it the call of their heart. So I too had to face this inner voice in my second test in the desert. It was my heart that I could hear again now that I had learned to control my thoughts and not let them lead me into the abyss." Expectantly

Tom looked at the dream interpreter. But the latter was silent, and gazed wearily at him. Tom noticed the sadness in his look, too, and wondered anxiously if the old man was feeling alright. Perhaps he was finding it hard to come to terms with the fact that Tom had already come up himself with the interpretation of his dream. Maybe he didn't feel needed anymore, now that he was getting older and his strength was slowly fading. Or maybe he needed money urgently and was dependent on the reward he wanted to claim from Tom for his dream interpretation one day. *I'll give him some money right after. After all, he interpreted my first dream and so I learned from him how to recognize the message of my dreams myself.* That it might be the heart stone the dream interpreter coveted at the end no longer occurred to Tom. His life had long since ceased to be guided by the thoughts that had once inspired distrust and fear in him. Tom thought of Juanita and proceeded to tell the dream interpreter of the insight he thought he could interpret from his last dream.

"Even when the voice of my heart kept asking me to leave in my dreams, I was just wandering aimlessly in the desert. I didn't know what I was looking for. Eternities passed, and so I would have endlessly crossed the desert without making any progress, if I had not understood in the end what this test was about. In dreams, I had already known. In life, I didn't know until I met Juanita." He smiled. It was a smile as only love can conjure. "The universe has shown me that things sometimes just work out. Life always has a plan you can count on. There may be detours in store and times when things are dark." Tom's smile had turned into a glow. "But in the end, after the darkest hour, the sun appears and shows you the way. I didn't know at first where my path would take me after I repaired the finca and had all my options open again. I finally had enough money to return home to my old life. But every other destination was open to me as well, only I didn't know what my destiny was. It was at that very moment that the universe sent me Juanita." Tom felt his heart leap at her name. "It showed me that all I had to do was stay where I was and the happiness of the world would come to me on its own."

The dream interpreter wanted to say something. It seemed to Tom as if he was writhing in pain a little. *Maybe he's very worried about having forfeited his right to a reward, now that I'm so good at interpreting my dream on my own. Maybe he's worried about money after leaving Nepanthé, and doesn't even know how to pay for his food.* Tom decided to invite him. Afterwards, he would even give him a considerable part of his money, which he no longer needed now and which the dream interpreter seemed to have so much more need of since Tom saw really deep sorrow and anxiety on the latter's face.

But Tom dared not to ask about it, not wishing to embarrass the old man, and instead concluded his remarks: "In my dream, I had already made up my mind not to ride into the desert the next day but to wait under the palm tree for what the universe had in store for me." Tom paused. "Then Juanita came into my life. Through her, I came to understand that the universe reveals the purpose of existence to man all by itself, when the time is right, without the need to search for it. Juanita is my purpose in life. I have finally found the answer to the question that once led me to Nepanthé and to you." Tom smiled. He had never felt so happy. All the agony and toil of the past had been worth it. He remembered how desperate he had been after losing his fortune. He thought of the disorientation with which he had come to this country before he had been given the gift of carelessness in Nepanthé. Even his father's death he could suddenly see from a different perspective. *In the end, it was he who led me here. Without him, I would never have met Juanita.* Tom thought of his stone. *Your stone already knows the way.* The dream interpreter had prophesied that at the very beginning of their encounter. "I am grateful to you for all you have done for me," Tom said to the old man. He was about to take out the money when the old man made him pause. "That's alright," said the dream interpreter. "Your thanks are enough for me today." *He is certainly ashamed,* Tom thought regretful. But before he could even get the check and slip him some money, the old man had gotten up, paid his obolus on the front counter, and disappeared.

Chapter 24

Tom had wondered about the dream interpreter's quick departure. He sat at the small table outside the restaurant for a bit longer, thinking about it. While he drank his wine and remembered his encounters with this old man, he noticed that the dream interpreter had always disappeared after each of their conversations. In Nepanthé he had sent Tom away. After the evening by the fireside, he had sneaked out. Tom had the feeling that he had almost fled from him, so quickly had the dream interpreter left this time.

He must be in big trouble, Tom thought, regretting that he hadn't found a way to help. *Perhaps the dream interpretation business isn't developing like it used to.* Tom thought about his old life for a moment and could imagine that times weren't as easy for dream interpreters anymore. Fewer and fewer people acknowledged their dreams. If they still dreamed at all. Tom could understand that. He, too, had stopped dreaming until he came to Nepanthé. And if the few who had their dreams interpreted at first ended up being good at it on their own, there wasn't much business left for a dream interpreter in this world.

Tom noticed he was getting tired. The wine didn't go well with the midday heat. In the past, he would have been suspicious and believed that the dream interpreter had poured something into his glass. But today, he only rejoiced in the rising midday heaviness. He thought of Juanita and was glad that he had understood how to pass his final test in the desert. And while he wondered about his next meeting with the donkey and the Bedouin, he fell asleep and began to dream again.

Chapter 25

The sun shone on Ala K'ins closed eyes. He had to blink, and after a while he realized where he was. Again, he had woken up under the palm tree, like so many times before. Again, he lay in the shade that cooled him a little, and again he waited to hear the voice and to meet his supply-packed donkey.

But something was different from all the other mornings he had already lived through. Something deep inside of him had changed since he had crossed the desert those countless times without knowing what he was actually looking for. Ala K'in remembered how he first had been puzzled when he woke up over and over again under this palm tree when starting his journey. At first he had seen it as a chance to take a new path. He could make a new attempt to reach his destination, which he did not know at all yet. Over time, he had gotten so accustomed to set out from this place in search of something he didn't know what it was supposed to be that he no longer questioned why it always led him back to this place.

On the contrary, he had quickly focused on finding the right way. Ala K'in had spent all his energy trying different approaches. A few times he had let his donkey, which he occasionally credited with the voice that spoke to him, decide. Other times he had led the donkey. He had approached the task systematically, trying to narrow down every possibility by first setting out in the various cardinal directions. But no way led him to his destination. There were days when he let chance decide, when he followed the direction of the wind or a sign he thought he had spotted in the sand. It was of no use. He had not been able to find the destination he didn't know yet in the years he seemed to be on the road.

At the moment when despair was at its peak, when he once again didn't know how to continue and when there wasn't anywhere to go, he remembered the origin of his journey.

"Aren't we leaving today?" he heard the voice ask. Ala K'in looked at his donkey. "It's about time that I give you a name," he said to the voice. "Since I know now who you are. I will call you Cormeum." He felt the voice nod in agreement. "That is a beautiful name," he heard it say. "I think it is a fitting name," Ala K'in said.

"So we're not leaving?" Cormeum asked again. "No, we are not setting out today, Cormeum." "Why not, Ala K'in?" the voice asked him, the donkey looking at him expectantly. His animal waited for him to settle on his back and lead him into the desert.

"You know, Cormeum, after all these travels, I realized one thing eventually." "What did you realize, Ala K'in?" asked Cormeum. Ala K'in sat down again in the shade of the palm tree and paused for quite a while. The words took a moment to form into a sentence what he already knew. The donkey watched, and Cormeum could see the pounding in Ala K'in's mind. There was a fire glowing as in a forge. Sparks were flying, and when Cormeum caught sight of one of them in Ala K'ins' eyes, the work was done. It was the phrase Ala K'in spoke now that was stated like a realization beaten into metal and that he consigned to impermanence when he uttered it, "Life is not a journey."

"What do you mean, Ala K'in?" asked Cormeum, and Ala K'in replied, "It is an illusion that we think we have to go somewhere, to seek a destination, to arrive somewhere." "But what is life like then?" asked Cormeum. "Life is like the music and the dance. We don't listen to the music to get to the end, and we don't dance to get to a certain place. We listen to the music for its own sake. We dance for the moment we are in dancing. We immerse ourselves in it and do not strive for a destination. A destination would only set us back once we reach it. It would start a new search for a new destination. Just as we begin over and over again each day to start our journey here at the palm tree."

Ala K'in had remembered last night that this was a test that had a purpose. He was in search of the meaning of life. That was his destination, which he had almost forgotten about while traveling through the desert. But the Bedouin had told him that in order to make progress in his search for the meaning of life, he had to dwell in the moment.

"So we will not be leaving today," Ala K'in said loud and clear. The donkey watched him for a while sitting in the palm tree's shade. Then the animal sat down too, stretched his head, and rested on the ground in the middle of the desert.

After they had rested like this for a while and after Ala K'in felt the contentment with which the donkey lay on the ground as well, and after watching the sand, Ala K'in suddenly heard the voice again.

"But tomorrow our supplies will be depleted. What will you do then, Ala K'in?" asked Cormeum. Ala K'in lingered in the shade of the palm tree, and the doubt in Cormeum's words had summoned thoughts that began to stalk Ala K'in. Like the siege of a fortress they were about to take, these thoughts buried themselves in the dunes that Ala K'in gazed upon. They prepared to strike at any moment and take possession of Ala K'in. But Ala K'in remembered his first test and saw the thoughts vanish with the desert wind soon. Completely grounded again, he thought, *So be it.* Ala K'in's heart beat calmly and peacefully, and when he heard the voice for the last time that day, it too was peaceful, repeating, "So be it." Ala K'in sat hour after hour in the shade under the palm tree. He did not drink, he did not eat. He only contemplated the world around him. The winds felt like music. And just before fatigue overcame him, he saw himself in the middle of the dunes. He danced, and fell asleep.

The next morning, he woke up in the same place where he had fallen asleep. When his mind was awake, Ala K'in opened his eyes. With clear vision he saw the sun, the sky and the desert. He sat once again in the shade of the palm tree. But the voice he heard this time was firm and clearly penetrated his ear.

"You see, my dear Ala K'in, you have made another step forward on your journey," said the Bedouin. In Lak'ech stood in front of him, and it seemed to Ala K'in as if he had never been away. As if he had fallen asleep here just yesterday, after he had looked into the mind mirror. As if his travels in the desert had been in a single dream that didn't want to end and from which he had awoken just now.

"There is one last test for you," In Lak'ech said, and his gaze grew dull and sad. Somewhere, Ala K'in had seen that look before. Someone he had met not so long ago had looked at him with that very worried gaze. As the sky darkened over the desert and gloomy clouds on the horizon heralded a storm that seemed to threaten all life, Ala K'in sensed that it would be the most difficult test of all.

Chapter 26

When Tom awoke from the dream he had sitting in front of the restaurant, it was late in the afternoon already. The restaurant owner had let him take his siesta at the table for a long time and had not awakened him. He knew the young man well by now and knew that he was a friend of the landowner and his daughter. But now he had to set the tables for the evening. Tom was grateful that he still had time to run some errands that Juanita had asked him to do. She seemed to be looking forward to a special evening with him. He had sensed that when she had sent him away. She was probably preparing something at the finca. Tom smiled.

But he also remembered his dream. He had been right. The universe sends you everything you need. There's no need to worry too much about the meaning of life. Brooding only leads you on endless journeys through the desert without getting closer to your destination. Sometimes it was enough to do nothing at all and let things happen. Meeting Juanita had made him realize that. Tom had arrived in life.

But there was something else at the end of the dream that he couldn't quite remember. It seemed to him that he had missed something. Something he had forgotten. Although his journey was complete after all, it seemed to him that his dream was still unfinished. But Tom couldn't explain it. He had met Juanita. His life had meaning now. Perhaps it meant to seal this bond for life. Tom sensed it would happen soon. His heart beat faster when he thought of telling each other's vows.

But that wasn't what irritated him. Something dark had awoken him from his last dream. He remembered that now. A shadow had settled over the lightheartedness that had surrounded him. Perhaps it had been only the strange, swift departure of the dream interpreter. Probably he was worried about the old man even in his dream. Tom decided not to follow thoughts that led him in a dark direction once again and pushed his feelings aside. Later he would see Juanita. And maybe he would ask her tonight.

Chapter 27

The dream interpreter had left the village in a hurry. Again he had seen too much in the boy. Just as he had once failed to see that darkness would obscure the boy's vision, it was joy now and maybe even love itself, that blinded the boy. This time he would really need the dream interpreter's help.

As the dream interpreter wandered across the meadows and fields, he already saw the shadow moving towards the finca. *Death always takes its toll when it sends one on a journey.* Should he perhaps have told the boy that after all, when he had first met him back in Nepanthé? Deeply saddened now, the dream interpreter now watched the dark make its way to the hill in the middle of the valley. He had wanted to warn the boy. But he knew that the course of events was not to be changed. *Things happen as they're supposed to happen.* He had no right to interfere with fate. He knew that in the end he even could not. What life had planned to happen was about to happen. The dream interpreter couldn't have stopped it.

The boy had forgotten that there were three tests he had to pass. He seemed so happy to have found the happiness that he overlooked the fact that his dream was not yet finished. The most difficult test was still to come. It was the one that broke most people. Like the landowner who never overcame the loss of his lands and who could no longer find the strength to rebuild the finca because it was not his real dream. The boy, too, had thought his dream was to find the one true love he had never known before. But that was a mistake. For love is self-sufficient. It is not bound to any dream of life. So the dream interpreter wondered if he should have told the boy about love.

Love outlasts death and does not disappear. *That's what makes it so painful,* the dream interpreter thought with deep regret. It is indelible. Love is beyond time and space. *We love people even when they are no longer with us.* The dream interpreter's heart grew heavy at this thought. Love is the universal artifact of the world soul. It links people. It can accompany them on their journey through life and be a good guide. It makes the heart speak to them. But it is not the purpose of life. Tom was about to learn all that. And it would be a painful task.

The dream interpreter was in great distress. He knew that it would be a matter of life and death for the boy as well this time. He didn't need fire, wind and ash to tell him this.

So he set about summoning the forces that worked in the world. He stood in the midst of the meadow he had wandered and paused. The dream interpreter closed his eyes and murmured the silent words of nature. He had to summon the butterflies.

Chapter 28

It was going to be a surprise. Juanita was so looking forward to it. She knew it had all started with the tractor. She still remembered her father coming home that night many months ago and telling her about it. Telling about the young man who had been able to fix the tractor. Telling that the finca would be rebuilt. Telling that his dream was coming true after all. She had never seen so much life in his face. From that day on, her father was changed. Just as he told her night after night about the finca's renovation, she also saw the colours coming back into his life. They made the gray that had surrounded him all these years disappear. Her father was coming back to life as well as the finca. So Juanita had liked the boy already long before she met him for the first time that night at the finca.

Juanita had never learned to operate a tractor. But she had always been self-educated in her whole life because she had to. She still remembered how she had climbed onto the big machine with a little trepidation when she and Tom took their first trip together. That night, however, she was determined to drive the tractor towards him all by herself at any cost.

Juanita had planned the evening for a long time. She had sent Tom to the village to have him run some errands for her. She herself would follow in the evening and meet him at the fountain in the marketplace. She imagined herself driving the tractor into the square and Tom noticing in amazement that it was her steering the big machine. She imagined his face, looking up at her proudly, loving her for teaching herself to drive. Just as she had always had to learn all things in life all by herself because there was no one to teach her.

Then she would drive with Tom to her favorite place. High up on the slopes of the almond tree mountain. There they would spend a special evening, at the end of which she would ask him a special question. Juanita had always had to manage her life all by herself. Now the time had come to share it with this boy who had brought magic back into her world. It was a magic she hadn't known since she was a little girl. A magic that was there before the dark days came and before her family fell apart and lost everything. Before her father faded and slowly collapsed just like the finca.

Now the magic was back, and Juanita dreamed of this new life. She thought about Tom. She pictured herself with him on the finca in the evening sun. They would have children and grow old together. Her heart was full of love. Juanita closed her eyes and imagined Tom looking at her after she had asked him the question. His overjoyed face shouting a loud laughing yes was the last thing on her mind. She died when the tractor slid into the ditch when it turned onto the main road, burying her underneath.

Chapter 29

Tom learned of her death when he returned to the finca in the evening. Still in the village, a feeling of heaviness had stirred in him. It had become a bad premonition as he made his way back. Panic-stricken he had rushed up to the finca when he saw the tractor in the ditch. His worst fears became a real nightmare when he learned what had happened.

They would have to inform the landowner, he was told, but then he got in shock. They left him alone on the terrace. He wanted to be on his own now, was the only thing he had been able to say.

Tom's heart felt like it had been ripped out. Where it had once beaten, was only an aching emptiness. It was a void that ached endlessly. That pain was the only thing Tom felt left of life. He didn't know what to think anymore. He didn't know how to feel anymore. He had no strength left. His soul was in shambles. All over the finca were its traces. The soul shards were scattered all over the property. They were stuck in the timbers of the barn and in the wreckage of the tractor. They lined the path and the hedges, the flowers, and almond trees. They shattered the path at the bottom of the steps where Tom had first seen the beautiful girl.

The picture of her standing on the terrace, bathed in the evening sun, and smiling, cracked in his thoughts. Everything that had given new life to his soul died with this moment.

Tom sat on the terrace and stared. His empty gaze was fixed on the valley, and even that empty gaze caused him pain. *Once the universe decides to take everything from you, there is nothing you could do about it.* Those were his thoughts. Tom tried to imagine, briefly, that it might be a natural cycle. *As there is inhalation, so there is exhalation.* That is the condition of life. The universe gives. Nepanthé, the finca, love for the girl. Then it takes its toll. But the toll Tom was paying right now felt like the exhale after the last breath.

The open box with the heart stone was beside him. Tom glanced wearily at the crystal. Its sharp edges flashed in the sun. He remembered hurting himself by touching the stone back then. It had been the first night at this finca, and even in his nightmare, he had felt the injury. The wound had healed, the abyss had vanished from his nightmare, and Tom had been able to free himself from all evil. *But this wound will never heal.* There is something final about death. Tom thought briefly of how he had felt after his father's death. His life had fallen apart then, too, and he had been lost. But his life at that time was a backdrop. The girl's death crashed a life that wanted to be lived. It had meaning and joy and a future. But she was dead now. *That wound can never heal.* Tom looked again at his stone. *You were supposed to protect me. But just like back then you betrayed me.* Tom remembered that after he cut his hand, he had thought the stone might be two-faced. But what he thought now was far worse. *The stone protects you. If it's with you, everything will be fine.* That was what his father had always told him. *It was a lie.* His father had left him nothing but a lie. The lie of believing in a world of magic and wonder. A world where dreams could come true if he persisted in following them, and where anything he imagined would come true. *It was a lie.* Bitter tears streamed down Tom's face. They were tears of anger and despair. *Life is a lie.* And there was no meaning in it either. If there was joy, it was only there so that suffering could be felt. *The stone is a lie.*

With that thought, the darkness entered Tom's mind. It encouraged him to follow that thought. It reinforced it. Of course, the stone was a lie. *Your father left you nothing but lies.* Nepanthé, the dream interpreter, places of carelessness and love were all lies to make the truth that life held seem all the more painful. There was no meaning. The universe didn't care about life. It was a bad joke made up by someone who didn't even care if he laughed at it or not. Any attempt by figures like the dream interpreter to imbue life with something mystical only led to a mirage designed to distract him from this sad truth. And then the darkness gave Tom a far worse thought. *I will prove it to be a lie.* Tom's gaze, which had rested lifelessly on the box, was now focussed on the stone. Sharp and dangerous, its edges flashed in the sun's rays. The point, which Tom's father had always called the magic part of a prism, sparkled menacingly in the sun like a green dagger. *I'll prove it. This stone will not protect me.* And with that thought, Tom reached for the crystal. As tightly as he could he grabbed it. Blood trickled off his fingers. In his mind, Tom had already held the stone high into the sky. *It's a lie,* the darkness whispered louder and louder. *Show your so-called heart stone where your heart is,* it whispered in Tom's mind. His inner eye saw the bleeding dagger drive into his chest and shatter the last remnant of his soul. The moment the stone entered his heart, the lies would stop and everything would come to an end. Tom had already imagined this rush into that future. He saw himself falling to the ground and his body and blood melting into the finca's floor. Forever he would be linked to this place. Time would pass and ruin the finca again. Tom's mind would not stop searching desperately for the beautiful girl he once wanted to spend his life with here. But he wouldn't find her. The pain in his hand led Tom's gaze back to the stone he held clutched in the box. *It's a lie. End it!* the darkness commanded. A gloomy look that had taken possession of Tom and that was no longer his own concentrated entirely on the sharp stone in his hand. Just as he was about to raise it up into the sky, it happened. Something had perched on the tip of the crystal. It was a butterfly.

In hot tears that were a mixture of hope and exhaustion, Tom let go of the stone. He sank down in the chair. Sunrays settled on his burning eyes like a warm cloth. They made him close his eyes and fall weak and weary into a long and deep sleep.

Chapter 30

"What kind of test is this?" asked Ala K'in concerned as he saw the gloomy clouds in the sky. In Lak'ech looked towards the darkness, which now seemed to spread more and more across the desert. "See for yourself," the Bedouin spoke, pointing to the darkness that was rapidly approaching and seemed to swallow everything.

Ala K'in looked into the dark void and was terrified. Although he had learned to stop thinking bad things, what he saw was so terrifying that it threatened to take complete possession of him. It was a huge black hole, sucking in whatever it found in the desert. A moment ago it had been on the horizon. But it spread quickly and grew larger. The longer and deeper Ala K'in stared into this nothingness, the faster it sucked in everything it came in contact with. The sky collapsed in pieces just as the sand was sucked into the hole, creating a massive storm. Ala K'in noticed how the dark nothingness grew stronger and stronger, threatening to take him as well. The last sunrays were just being swallowed up by the darkness, when he asked In Lak'ech loudly in the midst of the storm, "What is this? Where did this darkness come from?" The storm tugged at the Bedouin. His robes fluttered in the wind. "You brought it here," he shouted back. "It is your longing for death." Ala K'in had not been able to say the last words, so loudly did the storm roar around them. The palm tree snapped off and flew into the hole taking a huge curve. The darkness took the donkey as well, and Ala K'in watched in horror how his animal also disappeared into the darkness. "What shall I do?" cried Ala K'in. Sand was everywhere, and Ala K'in could barely spot the Bedouin. He fell onto his knees, still watching In Lak'ech standing bolt upright in front of him. As the black hole got closer and closer in the background and finally engulfed the entire horizon behind the Bedouin, In Lak'ech was first swept straight up into the air and then swallowed by the eternal black of that raging storm. "In Lak'ech," Ala K'in shouted at the top of his lungs. He let go of all hope and it seemed as if all his courage disappeared into that hole. He felt his soul losing its grip, hurtling into the darkness, though his body still crouched on the desert ground. Now, everything around him was black. In that last moment, just as he was about to close his eyes and let the eternal darkness wash over him, he saw it: a flash in the black hole. It was only a brief spark. Ala K'in could barely figure out where it came from or what it was. Straining, he focussed his gaze firmly into the black to find that bright spark. Sure enough, as he fixed the darkness with all his remaining strength, it flashed once more. And once more, and then faster and bigger. Amidst the darkness was something growing larger and visible in its outline. It sparkled and shone. It was as if a glimmer of hope was born, displacing the black from which it finally emerged.

The storm slowly subsided. The sand settled again, and the blue sky returned. The sun's rays began to shine again, and as that thing Ala K'in had first seen as a small glimmer of hope on the black horizon loomed in front of him, the palm tree and his donkey had also returned. "Now you recognize it," he heard the Bedouin's voice. In Lak'ech stood quietly beside him again as the sparkling object stood in all its beauty in front of them in the midst of the desert. It was a huge green crystal, rising out of the desert sands high up into the sky, and it gave Ala K'ins world a brilliant color.

Ala K'in thought he had seen something like it before, although nothing of this size. But as the sun rose in the sky above the crystal and the rays of light refracted a little differently, Ala K'in realized what it was: it was a massive prism of solid glass, opening up in the shape of a giant pyramid.

"That is where you have to go and find the center," In Lak'ech said. Ala K'in looked at him and then back at the pyramid, inside of which different colors created by the sun were gradually beginning to unfold. Fascinated, Ala K'in watched the spectacle and the beautiful rays of light that created entire rooms and halls inside the pyramid. "Where can I find the entrance?" asked Ala K'in after a while. But he realized soon that he had asked into the void, for In Lak'ech had once again silently disappeared.

When the midday sun at its peak above the huge prism, it turned the light play of colors into a storm of bright green, blue, yellow, and red, as if rubies and emeralds were all over the pyramid's passages and chambers, showing their floors and walls. Ala K'in could see everything that was being created inside the pyramid from the outside through the glass. His gaze fell upon the last refracted rays of light that now reached the bottom of the prism, and amidst the forming contours of rainbow colors he saw the great entrance. It was a portal that became visible at the base of the pyramid.

"Let's enter," Cormeum said, and without turning around he noticed his donkey first behind him and then by his side. Calm and considered, Ala K'in mounted and rode step by step towards the entrance. The steps to the portal seemed endless. Ruby reds alternated with opal blues, emerald greens, and golden yellows. Everything was crystalline, and when they finally reached the top, a portal opened up that looked as if it led directly into a rainbow.

Ala K'in hesitated for a moment before he entered. The colors were warm and friendly, but he also sensed that they had a downside. It was an energy that could also reverse itself if the colors didn't flow in the right direction, and then turn against you. "Shall we dare, Cormeum?" he asked the voice. Immediately his donkey strode inch by inch towards the entrance, and it was not long before Ala K'in and his animal had disappeared into that world of color.

Ala K'in could not tell how long they had been riding inside the pyramid already. For what his donkey and he found there felt like a vast labyrinth. Each corridor was bathed in a different light and was a different color. When he rode down one of the hallways, Ala K'in felt the energy of the colors connect with him and release something within him. As if inner vortices of energy were being triggered, which Ala K'in seemed to know from ancient lore. There were seven of them in number. "In this pyramid, I experience myself," Ala K'in thought, realizing that these colored corridors he rode through were his own inner points of energy. *Then I must be on the right path,* he thought, thinking of the Bedouin's words. *You have to find the center.*

Ala K'in noticed that the energies made him feel good when he was on the right path. In the red corridors, he felt warmth and safety. He felt connected to Mother Earth and had the comforting thought of being a child of this world. However, if he rode the wrong path, the energy had a reverse effect. Ala K'in then felt almost off balance on his donkey. He struggled to keep himself upright. Security was suddenly replaced by fear, and connection was replaced by the worry of being alone and lost in this world. But Ala K'in had learned to live in the moment, and so on the one hand he enjoyed the pleasant feelings the color energies produced, and on the other he was able to bear the unpleasant feelings with an inner serenity. By listening so deeply and mindfully to himself, he developed a sense of when he was on the right path in this labyrinth and when he needed to correct his path. Thus his donkey and he rode for quite a while through the corridors of the labyrinth, and Ala K'in experienced all the splendor and terror of his human emotions. All the while, however, he sat quietly and peacefully on his donkey. Sometimes, when he was completely absorbed in the moment, it seemed to him as if he had experienced this riding on the donkey before. As if there was something deep inside of him that he had once known as truth, but had forgotten again.

They had been riding like this through the endless corridors of the colored pyramid prism for quite some time when Ala K'in sensed that they were close to the end. He gradually recognized the corridors by their energy and avoided riding in the wrong direction more and more often. So he realized soon that all the energies in his body were in perfect harmony now. At that moment, he saw a figure at the end of the corridor, enveloped in glaring light. Joyfully at having finally arrived, he rode towards this person. But as he and his donkey left their path, he was astonished to find out that he was outside of the pyramid again. Once again he stood in front of the entrance. The glare he had seen was the sunlight and the person standing at the entrance at the top of the steps was the Bedouin. "You have to go to the center," the Bedouin said again. Ala K'in didn't quite understand. He had actually thought he had reached his destination, after all. What had he missed? So Ala K'in turned around and entered once again the pyramid. But again he found himself at the entrance after a while, and again In Lak'ech urged him to find the center. Ala K'in tried everything his mind could think of to take the right path through the labyrinth. He faced the energies that led to the most terrifying feelings within him as much as he tried not to let the joys turn into frolic when he rode through the corridors in perfect harmony with the colors. But it was of no use. In the end, every path led him back to the portal and to the Bedouin who spoke the significant words.

Ala K'in was about to give up. The sun was setting and the colors of the prism pyramid were fading. But then something revealed itself above the portal, which Ala K'in had overlooked so far every time he had passed the entrance with his donkey. It was words carved into the archway above the portal that Ala K'in struggled to decode. When he saw what was written there, he understood his task. His gaze wandered to In Lak'ech, who stood directly in front of the gateway now, the setting desert sun shining behind him as if in a mirror.

"Now you realize it," the Bedouin smiled gently. "There is only one way to go from here." Ala K'in nodded. "That path you have to continue by yourself." Ala K'in felt a little wistfulness when he heard those words. He tried to not get sad, and yet he felt a small but warm ache spreading through his body ever so gently. "It will pass," In Lak'ech said. "It's not a real goodbye, after all. Let's shake hands." With those words, In Lak'ech held out both of his hands, and Ala K'in wanted to grasp them with his own. But as he reached for In Lak'ech's hands, he saw his fingers disappear into those of the Bedouin, quite as if they were dipping into a lake. It seemed to him that he was melting into his own reflection. Then his arms also disappeared into In Lak'ech's arms. As he melted into the Bedouin, he looked into his face one last time. As a farewell, Ala

K'in was left with only one last gesture of humility. Tilting his head slightly forward, he said, "Now then, In Lak'ech..." "Ala K'in, it has been a great pleasure," the Bedouin returned, and as through his reflection, Ala K'in went through him. And now he remembered who he really was.

As the sun got nearer to the horizon, the words above the portal's archway slowly disappeared. Carved in stone, there was written in one of mankind's oldest languages: In Lak'ech Ala K'in.

Chapter 31

Tom's eyes snapped open. Someone was about to shake him awake. He looked up into a startled face. "Boy, what's the matter with you? Are you alright?" The landowner stood in front of him, pale as a corpse. His eyes fell on Tom's hand. As Tom followed that gaze, he noticed that his hand was hanging over the armchair beside him, covered in blood.

He woke up slowly and realized that, after the events of the day, the slumped sight of him with a bloodied hand in an armchair on the porch must have caused terrible apprehension in anyone who found him like that. Instantly he became aware that the death of his beautiful girl was real. Immediately he felt a stab in his heart. But before the feeling could take over, he pulled himself together for a moment. He didn't want to upset her father anymore. *She wouldn't have wanted that.* "It's all right," he reassured the landowner, still a little dazed. "I just cut myself badly and probably lost consciousness. I can't see any blood." At the last words, he noticed the landowner struggling with tears. Images of the tractor came to Tom's mind and he couldn't help but think of how the girl had been killed by it. Tears welled up in Tom's eyes as well, and the landowner immediately saw what Tom was thinking of. He broke in front of him. Like a little boy he buried his face in Tom's lap, and Tom bowed his head over him. He, too, began to cry. For a while, they huddled together like that. They had both lost the most important person in their lives. They both felt guilty. Without their meeting and the finca, there would have been no tractor. They both cursed themselves for it. When they looked at each other again, the same question came up. Why hadn't they been able to let go of their dream?

"Because dreams always require sacrifice," they suddenly heard a voice say. Standing on the porch, as if from nowhere, was the dream interpreter. He was glad to see the boy alive. At least this time he hadn't been too late.

"You never told me what sacrifice I have to make for my dream," Tom heard the landowner say to the dream interpreter in a quivering voice. Did he, too, know the old man? The dream interpreter noticed Tom's questioning look. "I am attracted to all dreams, even the wrong ones," he said, turning to Tom as if reading his mind again.

Now the landowner noticed that the dream interpreter knew the boy as well. "Did he send you on such a cursed journey as well?" The tremor in his voice had grown louder. Anger mingled with it. Tom nodded. They both turned to the dream interpreter with a demanding look.

"It is in your own hands whether you face your final test, or whether you fail forever, like that one," said the dream interpreter to Tom. The old man pointed sternly at the landowner, and without waiting for a response, he spoke. "If you give up now, you will be like him. You will betray your dream, and only that betrayal will expose it as a false dream. But if you pass even this test, what you have striven for will be fulfilled." Tom noticed how he began to think about the words of the dream interpreter.

"Get out of here!" the landowner shouted at the dream interpreter. "You have brought me nothing but misfortune! " The dream interpreter looked at him pityingly. "No, you did that all by yourself." He looked at him firmly. "He who begins a dream has to end it. If you cannot, you will inevitably fail. And for that failure, you are entirely responsible." Tom saw something mingle in the landowner's gaze at these words that he already knew. "You promised me a finca from which I could one day overlook my entire estate. And now my daughter is dead!" Tom felt darkness spread through the landowner that he had just been carrying himself. "You have deceived me," the landowner's rage now increased. *You have deceived me,* it echoed in Tom's mind. Had he not thought so himself just a moment ago? Tom's face changed. He reached for his box and put it, with the stone inside, into his pocket. In the landowner's face, he saw something gloomy. It was darkness. He must have looked like that himself when he was just struggling for his life with the stone in his hand. Tom looked at his cut and felt horror rise within him as he noticed how the landowner, in his anger, let more and more of the darkness in.

"Look at it, my boy," said the dream interpreter. "He could not follow his dream. Now he will not even blame himself for it." Tom looked sadly and wistfully at the landowner, to whom he had been so long bound in friendship. He was about to say something, but when the landowner saw Tom in his thoughts, he roared at the boy in the same way, "You can go away, too!" And if that wasn't enough, he followed it up with, "Because of you, my daughter is dead!" Tom was stung by the words. He saw the look on the landowner's face that was no longer his own. And in his rage, the landowner now uttered something that destroyed forever all that had been between them, "Your tractor killed her. You are a murderer!" At those words, the bond that had linked the two men since Tom had given this old estate a life again, broke. Thoughts can send disaster, but words are eternal. Nothing would be the same between them. If they had been united in grief a moment ago, those words had made them strangers.

The dream interpreter had long since left with the boy when the landowner was still cowering on his porch, full of rage and tears. Hatred and darkness had poisoned his heart. But more than the boy, the dream interpreter, or anything else in the world, he hated himself above all. So the finca became a place of darkness, where henceforth the unfulfilled dreams of men gathered and broke upon themselves.

Chapter 32

"What can I do now?" With a silence still mingled with a deep sadness, Tom looked at the dream interpreter. For a long time they had wandered together aimlessly over meadows and fields. The finca was far away already, almost as if it belonged to another life.

"You can go anywhere from here," said the old man, after they had been silent for a while. They had left the meadows and fields behind them and had wandered along endless paths until their way led them to a small place with a foundling in the middle. Tom sat down on this stone to rest a little. The old man stood quietly before him, gazing out into the world. The path forked at this point. When Tom looked more closely, he noticed that there were several paths that crossed here. The old man was right. Any path could be taken from here.

"But there isn't any path left for me to choose." Tom looked into the dream interpreter's eyes. He hadn't lost his will to live nor had he lost his direction. He had come to a point in his life where there was no path anymore. He could neither live nor die. He had no strength to hate or to love. He could not drift or seek a destination. He could no longer sink into the moment. He threatened to freeze inside.

"There is only one way left to go when there are no other ways," said the dream interpreter. Tom looked around. He saw the many forks. He imagined where their paths would lead him. Sometimes he saw himself as a broken man, a landowner on a finca lapsing into torpor and bitterness. Other times, a path would lead him back to his old life. Every day, he'd spend burying his memory and not allowing for a future. The daily routine would be torture instead of immersion. He would put his life behind him and end up wishing he had ended it on the finca porch many years before when he still had the strength. A third path sent him on his journey once again. He would try to return to Nepanthé to taste the wine again and feel the carelessness. But the wine would be stale, and the bitterness within him would dull the carelessness he could never feel again as he had back then. His life would be one repetition, condemning him to make the same mistakes over and over again. He would feel some joy though and maybe taste some love again. He would feel sadness and despair at times. But no matter what he felt, each time it would only be a faint copy of what he had once felt. He would watch himself fade away until he would be completely transparent eventually. His disappearance at the end of life would be so insignificant that neither he nor anyone else would really notice.

So every way he looked at led to a path that seemed so hopeless that Tom sat on his little boulder not able to move. He threatened to turn to stone himself. *I might melt into this little boulder on which I now sit, and become one with it. I might become a signpost to the wanderers who pass this way. For I know every path that leads away from here.* For a moment, he liked the idea of sitting here eternally and showing the way to those who pass by. *Then perhaps my life would have been worthwhile after all. I could show everyone what to expect. My experiences led everyone down a different path that seemed right to them.* But Tom knew that all paths led astray. They were detours that led every passing wanderer only to one of the lives he already had lived and which also hadn't brought Tom to his destination. *I would be a signpost into false dreams.*

"I never taught you to read the signs," said the dream interpreter suddenly, interrupting Tom's thoughts. Tom looked up. He had followed the butterflies and had believed that he would be able to interpret his own dreams in the end. But what he recognized as signs had often proved to be wrong. The thoughts he had during his first test had fooled him as much as the love he had felt for Juanita. They had even made him forget that his journey wasn't over yet.

"For your third test you will need the signs," the dream interpreter continued. Tom looked at him questioningly. "They are very close. You only have to follow them." Tom looked down and discovered something on the boulder on which he had been sitting all this time. It wasn't writing, but a figure of some sort. Tom thought at first he recognized a fossil that resembled a butterfly. But then he realized that he was wrong again. It looked familiar, but the boulder showed something else. Tom got up and stood in front of it. Then he clearly saw what was chiseled in the stone. It was a shell.

"You have to follow them until you arrive at the church," he heard the dream interpreter say. "I will be waiting for you at the end of this last path." When Tom turned around, the dream interpreter had disappeared. This time he had not sent Tom away as he had done in Nepanthé. He hadn't skulked off as after the evening by the fireside, and he had not fled as after the last encounter in the little restaurant. This time it seemed to Tom that the dream interpreter had dissolved just as the Bedouin had in his dream.

Tom looked at the shell and knew the old man was right. *You have to go to the center.* That was the test he had yet to face. He had experienced the moment and learned aimlessness. Both would help him on this final journey. He took one of the large branches from the ground and whittled himself a staff. Then he set out to reach Santiago de Compostela and entered the Way of Saint James.

Chapter 33

"Who are you?" Tom had wandered hundreds of miles before he heard that question. The path asked it. It was the only question the trail knew, and it asked it of everyone who walked it. Tom, however, had no answer.

His long journey had taken him from Seville via Salamanca to Ourense. Eternal solitudes he had put behind him. Again and again, he remembered his last dream. Just as he had experienced all the colours of his inner energies in the labyrinth of the glass pyramid the path made his inner being shine. The path connected him to Mother Earth and made him feel his life energy. It brought back his intuition and inner and outer clarity. The path made him listen to the voice of his heart and speak to his soul. Tom remembered how at the very end of his dream he had learned that there was no difference between the Bedouin and him. *Everything was inside of him, and inside of him, there was everything. The world outside is the world inside,* Tom thought. *Above as below.*

But Tom had not dreamed anymore. Perhaps he hadn't because he was waiting for it. Maybe his dream denied him the knowledge because he hadn't found it yet. *Who are you?* Did he have to answer that question to get to the center? Or did the answer lie in the center Tom was supposed to find in his dream?

One evening, he stopped for a rest and looked at his stone in the little box while sitting in the light of the campfire. Another hundred kilometers to get to Santiago de Compostela. Tom had only a few nights left to dream once again before he got there. *Your stone already knows where your path will take you. How can you not know when he already does?* That's what the old man had told him back in Nepanthé. He had been right about everything. Tom looked deep into the green crystal. *So, my heart stone, tell me: who am I?* Tom waited for a sign, for any answer.

"Can I join you?" A male voice suddenly spoke behind him. Startled, Tom flinched and made the box disappear quickly into his coat. He turned and was about to get up when the stranger asked him to remain seated. "I didn't mean to startle you, I'm sorry." A middle-aged man stood in front of him. He didn't look like he was from around here. He was a pilgrim, too. His pale skin and almost blond hair suggested he was from the north. Tom also thought he could hear an appropriate accent in the few sentences. It turned out that the man was Dutch. He introduced himself to Tom and told him that he too was on his way to Santiago de Compostela. Tom wasn't really in the mood for conversation, but he didn't want to be rude either. This man was the first person he had met on the way in a long time. He had met most of the pilgrims when they were close to the larger towns and villages.

But since he had decided early on to spend the warm summer nights out in the open rather than in one of the hostels, he was hardly used to company. Tom had hoped to better find himself this way and to pass his last test. But maybe now close to the end of the road, the universe was sending him someone to help him with his final task.

"What brings you to the Way of St. James?" asked the Dutchman, and after Tom had hesitated a little, he began to tell the man his story. The first evening he only told about his strokes of fate. But after they decided to walk part of the way together the next day, Tom also told about his other experiences and how he had fared on the finca. The Dutchman, for his part, told Tom that he was born into a very wealthy family and had grown wearier of the material things in his life. He longed for meaning and spirituality and didn't know anything to do with himself other than to walk the road to Santiago de Compostela eventually. When they had been walking together for almost three days, Tom asked the man about his dreams. The Dutchman didn't seem to quite understand at first until Tom told him about Nepanthé, the dream interpreter, and his own dreams. "It has happened to me quite the same way," the man said with a sigh. "Ever since I came to this land my dreams have led me on a journey to the meaning of my existence. I, too, have been wondering who I really am." Tom was momentarily puzzled that the Dutchman had such a similar dream. But probably many of the people he could meet here on the Way of

St. James were touched by the same questions that were troubling Tom.

"I have a treasure to guide me," said the Dutchman, as they sat together by the fire on the third evening. Tom looked at him expectantly. "It is a red ruby. An old heirloom from my family that my grandmother attributed magical powers to," the man explained. "I, too, have such a crystal," Tom said happily. He couldn't believe there were other people who were guided by stones. But probably that was the point of this path. You met people with similar fates and maybe could learn from them. The universe had sent Tom this man to assist him in his final test. "What kind of crystal do you have?" the Dutchman asked, and Tom briefly felt suspicious. It was the way the man suddenly asked, but Tom quickly blamed it on his accent. He had learned, after all, not to give too much credit to his thoughts, since they had so often led him astray. Distrust was no longer to rule Tom's world. After some hesitation, he told the man about the emerald his father had left him. He told of the *Tabula Smaragdina*, which the man surprisingly never heard of before, and what mysticism he also saw in his stone. Still, Tom was glad the Dutchman didn't ask him to take out the box. *He probably doesn't want to show his ruby either,* Tom thought and the thought reassured him. Probably, as the son of a rich family, he had all too often had bad experiences in showing his possessions openly. He probably was especially cautious. After all, one often heard stories of crooks and thieves who knew how to take advantage of the credulity of some well-heeled pilgrims and rob them of their possessions. Nevertheless, Tom didn't forget to mention that his crystal would probably be only a worthless shard of glass. But by then the Dutchman was no longer listening very attentively. Tired, they both fell asleep by the campfire. The next day, they had to walk the last stage.

Chapter 34

When Tom woke up the next morning, the Dutchman had disappeared. Startled and confused, he felt for his box and didn't find it at first. Reassured, he finally realized that he must have put it in a different pocket than he remembered from the night before. He glanced inside it and looked at his stone with relief.

"How about some breakfast?" he suddenly heard the Dutchman say behind him. Again Tom had winced, having thought the man had left already. Somewhat ashamed, Tom saw that he had only gone to the nearest inn, which was not far from their night's camp and had brought fresh coffee and some pastry. "I woke up early and couldn't get back to sleep," said the Dutchman, seeing what Tom had been thinking. "Did you think I was up and away with your gem?" he asked him searchingly. Tom was quiet. The Dutchman laughed. "Don't worry, I understand. I've often felt the same way. When you're rich you're always afraid people are trying to steal from you. I don't blame you."

Relieved and a bit shameful, Tom nodded. He was glad about the Dutchman's reaction and began to like the man, who had sometimes seemed a bit strange.

I'm still far too suspicious, Tom thought to himself and resolved to listen to his thoughts less in the future.

They had breakfast and talked a little more. Then it was time to set off. If they walked a good part of the way today, only one more night and they would reach Santiago de Compostela. They walked silently, striving to make progress. Tom often looked at the Dutchman, wondering if the latter would help him in his final test. *He has already reminded me not to worry too much*, he thought. *Maybe something will happen today, and on this last night, I will have another dream that will conclude my journey.*

And indeed something happened that evening unexpectedly at the campfire. As the Dutchman and he sat by the fire eating their dinner, a little dark figure joined them. It was another pilgrim, from the far east. First, he seemed weird to Tom and the Dutchman. They were only a few miles from Santiago de Compostela, and it was not unusual for them to meet other people again. But this little figure made them feel very suspicious. Tom saw that the Dutchman was not at ease either. Though he had resolved to follow no more bad thoughts, he thought that he had every reason to be careful if his newfound friend was also a little suspicious. As the little man from the east left the camp for a brief moment to relieve himself, the Dutchman addressed Tom. "I hope he doesn't mean to rob us. I know such people. It would be rude to send him away for no reason, but I don't feel comfortable around him." Tom agreed and asked what they should do. "I think one of us ought to stay at the nearest inn tonight. We can't both go, or he may come with us, and possibly rob us there." "But what are we going to do with our gems?" asked Tom, knowing that they have to come up with something quickly before the little man was back. "One of us has to take them both, so they won't be here with him," said the Dutchman. Seeing how uncomfortable Tom got now, he asked confidentially, "Will you go, or shall I?" Now, Tom was relieved. *He would even trust me with his ruby,* he thought. Again, he felt ashamed, because for a fraction of a second he had imputed evil intentions to the Dutchman again. "You go." It sounded like an apology. He wanted to prove to the Dutchman and more importantly to himself, that he had truly overcome his bad thoughts and could be confident. "Alright, I'll meet you tomorrow morning right outside the inn. Then we'll have breakfast and hike the last bit to the church together." The Dutchman smiled. Tom was relieved. Perhaps this was the test he had yet to pass in finding himself. He had to gain confidence in this world. He took out his little box and gave it to the Dutchman. His most important asset Tom could entrust to the world. The world wasn't evil. Even though he had only known the Dutchman for a few days, the universe had seemingly sent him to make Tom see the world through different eyes from now on. It wasn't enough not having the box with the stone near him all the time, Tom had to be able to let go of it completely. So he was glad to see that the Dutchman kept it well with him. When the little man returned, the Dutchman said he didn't feel well, and that he would rather spend the night at an inn. As the Dutchman packed his things by the fire and disappeared with his stone, Tom smiled. He had shown himself and the world that he trusted it, and thus hoped to have taken another step towards himself. *The stone was still the thing that stood in my way. Breaking away from it might bring me closer to myself.* The little man was already asleep beside him snoring as Tom thought about the events of the last few days and started getting tired. He wondered a little that it had been so easy for him to give away his stone after all. Or had he been careless? After all, he would get it back the very next morning. *If I can't give it away even for one night, then I'll be bound to it forever,* Tom thought and remembered the landowner and his finca. But at the same time, this thought felt strange, because his stone was his guide. *How could he find himself without it?* he wondered when he was already half asleep. *You have to let go of the things you hold most dear to see if they will come back to you. Only then you can be sure of their love.* The thoughts chased through his head. *But how does that help me figure out who I am? Maybe going to the center is a step away from the center? ,* Tom thought. By then he was almost completely asleep. Was he about to find out who he really was? With that last thought, he fell asleep hearing the words once again, "Who are you?"

Chapter 35

The young man found himself in a forest clearing. Again, he didn't understand how he had gotten here, but this time it felt right. He remembered that he had recognized who the old Bedouin was and who had led him this far from the words above the arch at the entrance to the colored prism pyramid. The ancient words of an even more ancient language, the meaning of which the man remembered the moment he had read them over the archway, told him: "In Lak'ech Ala K'in – You are I and I am you." It was the confession of unity and uniqueness that existed in many cultures and ancient languages. The man thought he heard a piece of universal music in it as he read the words over the gate.

He felt that this place was the end of the journey he had set out on so long ago. He still couldn't remember who he was or what his name was. But it seemed clear now that it was actually meaningless. He remembered why he had come here in the first place. "To find an old truth that you once knew but then forgot," he heard the voice say, and as he looked around he saw his donkey.

"Yes, a truth of which I was not aware of back then, and yet have come to find here today, my dear

Cormeum," said the young man. Mildly, he looked at his donkey standing in the forest clearing. The image made him think. Something about it he already knew.

"I'm sure you'll find your truth," he suddenly heard a much gentler voice say out loud and clear. Turning around again, the young man saw a boy in the forest clearing as well, smiling at him. "Do you like my donkey?" The man looked at the animal in wonder. "This is your donkey?" he asked. "Well yes, but you know it is," replied the boy surprised.

"Come with me, I will help you find your truth," said the boy, after he had mount the donkey. Silently, they walked together into the forest. They saw meadows and rivers, flowers and forest animals. They passed lakes and mountains. The path seemed to encompass the world of an entire human lifetime. They were silent all the time. Then the butterflies danced. The young man saw them in the clearing from which they had set out. It was in front of them again. The butterflies danced over the meadow, the wind played a piece of soft music, and then the young man saw the other boys with their donkeys.

"There you are," said one of the other boys. "Let's get going." "I'll be with you in a minute," the boy said, turning to the young man once again, "I'll have to lead them, they won't ride off otherwise. They don't know the country around here as well as my donkey and I do." The boy pointed to the waiting group. "But I promised you I would find your truth, and I will keep that promise," the boy continued. "Here," the boy pointed to a spot in the middle of the meadow where the butterflies were dancing. "Sit there and take this." With those words, he handed the man a quill and paper and had him take a seat in the middle of the forest clearing. The young man did as the boy asked, and yet did not quite know what it all meant. He looked questioningly at the boy, who had climbed back onto his donkey already and was riding towards the head of the group.

"Write your truth down now," the boy called as he slowly made his way out of the forest clearing with the others. "How am I to do that?" asked the young man. "The butterflies will bring you luck," laughed the boy, already disappearing behind the first trees.

The man watched the group of donkeys until the last animal had left the forest clearing. Then he began to write. He remembered with each line that appeared on the page. Filled with deep, inner contentment, he jotted down word after word, line after line, not even noticing how he was about to write down his old truth.

A while had passed. The young man had almost finished writing when he saw the group of boys on their donkeys return. The little boy still led them. When the young man had just put his last word on paper, the little boy and his donkey stood in front of him again. They both smiled.

"What am I supposed to do with this now?" the man pointed questioningly at the paper that held his story. "Well, you have to hide it deep under the pyramid," said the little boy, pointing to a spot where the forest split in two. Completely astonished, the young man saw his crystal again blinking at him between the now two forests.

"Why should I do this?" asked the young man, as the light of the pyramid got even brighter. "So that the truth may not be lost," the boy said aloud. It was the last thing the young man heard. As the light got brighter and brighter, he opened his eyes and knew his dream was over.

Chapter 36

Tom awoke by the glare of the midday sun. When he opened his eyes he recognized he was alone. The little man had disappeared, and Tom was about to look for his little box when he remembered that he had given it to the Dutchman the night before.

In a hurry, he packed up his things. It was already late. They had wanted to meet for breakfast at the hostel, but the dream had kept Tom asleep for way too long. What had he been dreaming about? He could still remember everything quite clearly, except what he had written down in that clearing in the woods. *Who are you?* The dream gave him no answer. If only he could remember what truth he had written on that paper. He had to get back to his crystal. In his dream, he had hidden the truth within it. *So my stone does know the answer,* Tom thought.

Tom didn't manage to get to the hostel in time, but the Dutchman had certainly been waiting. Just as they had agreed on. Now they would have lunch together. Tom would tell the Dutchman about his dream and ask his stone again. Maybe they would manage to solve the riddle by joining forces. After all, the Dutchman was not inexperienced with mystical crystals. In the end, his ruby might help solve the mystery.

But Tom found no one at the inn. It was okay at first because he himself had slept through the morning and had not gotten up for breakfast. He wondered why the Dutchman hadn't come back to the camp when he didn't find Tom at the inn early in the morning. Perhaps he had thought Tom had already started off for Santiago de Compostela. Just as Tom was about to set out, he saw the little man. He had filled his bottle with water at the well next to the hostel. "Well, we were lucky," he said, but Tom didn't quite understand. "We almost stayed at the camp with that Dutchman, if he hadn't set out so unexpectedly," explained the little man to the astonished Tom. "They told me this morning at breakfast at the inn that there was a Dutchman on the road in the neighbourhood, pretending to be of the wealthy kind, and so gaining the confidence of the pilgrims." Tom started feeling sick. "Then he tricks the poor people into trusting him with their belongings and then runs away with it." Tom's face turned pale. "It's a good thing he didn't stay with us at the camp. You probably scared him off with your distrust," said the little man. "I, too, was displeased with your manner at first. But I could not afford the inn, and now I am glad you drove him away. I thank you for that." With these words, the little man went on his way, for it was now past noon, and he wished to finish his journey in time.

Tom collapsed. He dropped down on the steps in front of the inn and began to cry. Again, he had done everything wrong. Again, he hadn't understood the test. Worse than that. After all the trials, he had fallen for a simple thief and had recklessly given him the most precious thing he still possessed. The stone was meant to guide him. Now he would never know what his dream held for him. Without the stone, he could no longer know the truth he had hidden within his dream. Tom tried once again to remember what he had written down during his dream in the clearing in the woods. But he quickly realized that he would not remember without his stone. His thoughtlessness had tricked him this time. All was lost. Tom sat on the steps of the inn a few miles away from his destination, knowing that he couldn't finish this last walk.

Chapter 37

He had sat like that until the afternoon sun announced the evening. Two journeymen from the town came to the inn to stop. Tom could hear them talking as they approached the steps where Tom still sat.

"The poor fellow really thought he had found a mystical treasure," he heard one say. "How angry he got when my master, the jeweler, kept assuring him it was only a shard of glass." "He didn't even take the box with him when he got up and left?" the other asked. "He probably left in a panic because my master started asking him awkward questions," the first journeyman said now. "The man probably robbed some poor pilgrim. But in the end, he has been the victim himself. The stupid fellow actually falls for a piece of broken glass." Then they both laughed out loud.

Tom had been able to hear the conversation clearly. He asked the two about it and got confirmed what he had hoped to hear. Where this jeweler was, Tom asked, and the two showed him the way.

The little shop was on the outskirts of town. The jeweler was about to close when Tom, out of breath, rushed into his shop. "We are already closed," he was saying when Tom asked for the little box. "Do you still have it?" The jeweler looked up. He smiled. "So, you own this treasure," he said while pulling something out from under the counter. It was his box indeed. Tom was relieved to discover that. For a moment he had thought there had been a mix-up. But the box was clearly his. "You mean my worthless shard of glass." Tom looked questioningly at the jeweler. The jeweler had to grin again. "I drove that scoundrel away with that story," he said, smiling. "When you've been in business as long as I have, you can tell right away who's coming to you with stolen goods." He looked at Tom, and after a pause added, "And you can also tell who actually has a shard from the *Tabula Smaragdina to* call his own." Tom's eyes widened. "The little crystal is of great sentimental value to me above all things," he said carefully. He feared the jeweler might demand a high price for the box containing the stone. "Don't worry," the jeweler smiled. "I don't charge anything for the return. Anyone who owns such a valuable mystical jewel deserves all the help in the universe." Tom was still in shock. He couldn't say anything. Just a moment ago he had thought all was lost, but now fate had sent him to a man who said his heartstone was what his father had always seen in it. So there was magic in this world after all. Tom tried to keep calm. "Of course the sentimental value is infinitely greater." The jeweler broke the silence. "Whereas the material price is well worthy of consideration," he then added with a joyful smile. "Is there anything else I can do?" the jeweler asked, and added without waiting for an answer, "Because, as I said, we are actually closed." With these words, he handed Tom the box with the crystal and led him to the door. As they said goodbye, Tom looked at him with tearful eyes and said, "Thank you! For everything."

Chapter 38

Tom stood in front of the shop for a while, looking at his box. Only the ringing of the bells brought him back into reality. The evening sun covered the streets of the small town with a warm red, and Tom noticed the many people now and among them a lot of pilgrims, streaming through the streets. He stopped a man walking by and asked him, "Do you know what this town is called and how I can get to Santiago de Compostela from here?" The man looked at him in wonder. Then he laughed merrily. "The answer to your first question will take you there." Tom did not understand. "You are already in Santiago de Compostela. Come along, the church bells are ringing. Soon, the Holy Mass will begin."

Amazed, Tom went with the crowd to the large square. He let himself be pulled along by the happy souls who had finally arrived at their destination after their long journeys. The church in the square was a breathtaking sight. All the power of the way was concentrated in it. The energies that people carried to it made it glow with all colors, just like the crystal pyramid in his dream. The crowd pushed towards the entrance, and Tom went with it towards the church.

Here his path ended. He held his little box tightly in his hand. Just as he was about to begin to think how he should pass his last test, and what his dream had meant to tell him, he saw it. Standing next to the entrance of the church, the dream interpreter was smiling. Shortly after, Tom was standing right in front of him. "Good to see you again," the dream interpreter said laughing. Tom nodded silently. "So you made it." Tom said softly, "No. I almost just lost my crystal. But I didn't remember the truth I dreamed." The dream interpreter looked at him, tilted his head a bit, and smiled. "You're lucky. I can interpret dreams."

A little later they were sitting in a café in the church square. The dream interpreter had taken Tom aside and led him out of the crowd. Tom had told him about his experiences on the Way of St. James. He told him about the Dutchman and the jeweler and how he had got his stone back and that it was indeed valuable because it came from the *Tabula Smaragdina*. Then Tom described his last dream to the dream interpreter. When he had finished, he looked at him expectantly. "Can you tell me what it means? What truth did I once know and forget later? What is written on the note the boy made me write? And above all, who am I?"

The dream interpreter looked at the boy for a very long time. He had known the answer to all these questions since the moment he had first met him at the cypress tree in Nepanthé. After a long pause that seemed like an eternity to Tom, the dream interpreter took a deep breath and spoke, "It is now time for you to grant me my reward." Tom felt a little uneasiness rise within him at the dream interpreter's sentence. He had completely forgotten that the latter's services had not been for free. In Nepanthé, Tom had promised to grant him whatever the dream interpreter would later demand. The wise man had foreseen everything. He had known that the dream would reveal itself by degrees and that Tom would then need his help. Perhaps the cypress had told him when the wind from the tree whispered something into the dream interpreter's ear. By then, Tom hadn't worried about a payment he didn't know yet. After all, he had believed he had it in his own hands whether he would use the dream interpreter's services more than just one time. The bond that had developed between the two of them over time had made Tom forget that the dream interpreter would claim his reward eventually.

"What do you want?" asked Tom uncertainly. His hand felt for the little box. Once, he had feared the old man cared for his treasure only. Perhaps he already possessed all the pieces of the mythical emerald tablet, and Tom's stone was the last shard he was missing. Worried, his hand clutched the box with the stone inside. Although he was so close to his life's purpose now, the stone remained the only reminder of his father. Tom's heart missed a beat when he saw the old man pointing to his bag. "Give me the box," said the dream interpreter, and Tom felt the scrutinizing gaze that now rested upon him. The old man did indeed want his stone. Tom found himself thrown back to the stairs of the inn, where he had sat that afternoon still mourning for his stone. *What have I been doing?*

For the interpretation of dreams, he had sacrificed his heartstone. *How could that be?* Thoughts flickered briefly in Tom's mind. *Did he really have to give the old man his stone? Had he tricked him as the Dutchman had? Had his services really been rendered?* Finally, the interpretation of the last dream was still missing. "Tell me the meaning of my last dream first," Tom urged the old man. But that one only replied, "You have to give me the box first." The dream interpreter watched Tom struggling with himself. His entire past was in that box. All the memories, images, and experiences he had once had and loved.

But Tom knew that the dream interpreter was right. After all he had done for him, there was no doubt that he would decode the last part of Tom's dream. He had every right in the world to claim his reward in return. *Do ut des,* Tom thought. I give that you may give. It was an ancient law. If he didn't want to displease the universe, he couldn't break that law. Tom took out his box and looked at it. A while passed and the dream interpreter's eyes rested gently on the image that formed around Tom and his box with the green crystal inside.

It is usually the last test that people fail, the dream interpreter thought watching Tom. *They all pursue their life's dream until that one last unremarkable moment. It is the hour when the night is at its darkest. Just before the sun rises. Instead of appreciating the trust the universe has placed in them, they throw it away just in front of the finish line. Then all the effort was useless. They never see the sun rise because they no longer believed in it.*

Tom was looking at his box. He lingered in that moment. He had learned to control his thoughts. They could not harm him anymore. He was completely absorbed in the moment. He closed his eyes and felt himself holding the box containing his stone. All the images that held his father's magic merged into it. They became one with Tom, and Tom became one with them. He was part of it all. *In Lak'ech Ala K'in.* Those were the words Tom saw again in his mind's eye. He felt his connection to the world soul. He felt that it would always connect him inseparably to the time that was and the time that would be. With all the images and events. With all the other people he had met on his journey. With the old woman and the innkeeper in Nepanthé, with the landowner and his daughter, even with the Dutchman and the little man from the east, with the two journeymen and the jeweler. And, of course, with the dream interpreter. But at that moment he also felt the connection with something else. Tom felt inseparable from his father. He could feel him in that one moment. He felt who his father was and how he had lived. His father's life opened up to him as if it were his own. Tom knew then that he himself was a part of the universe and that the universe dwelt within him. It needed no stone to remind him of this.

In perfect peace, Tom opened his eyes. He looked kindly at the wise old man and gave him what he had asked for. As Tom let go of the box, he felt his peace settle over the entire world. Everything around him became bright and quiet.

The dream interpreter's joy could not have been greater. He accepted the box and opened it. For a moment he looked inside. Then he smiled. The last part fitted into the big picture. Just as he had once foreseen it. Back when he stood with Tom on the mountaintop in front of the cypress tree and the wind told him of a new miracle that only those who believe in it from the bottom of their hearts can accomplish.

To Tom's great surprise, the dream interpreter handed him back the opened box. Wasn't inside what he had expected? "Show me what you have hidden under the crystal. That is all I ask as a reward." Tom did not quite understand. He remembered his dream, but no longer the truth he had written down at the boy's behest. Was that not what the dream interpreter was yet to explain to him? Tom looked at the box. Briefly, he feared it might be empty. But the little green crystal sparkled at him. He had never quite taken it out since his father had left him the box. Back then, when he found it beside his father's bed, he still feared he might destroy the memory if he once touched the crystal. Because touching it might erase the feeling he had felt as a child when he had held the stone. Later he had cut himself on it, and that too showed him that he had better leave the jewel in the box. He did not even like to think of his attempt, after the girl's death, to tear the stone out forcefully and rush into unhappiness with it. But right now, Tom took it very slowly and naturally. The magic of the stone had long since passed to Tom, and now it was a beautiful stone, of which Tom needed no longer to be afraid of. As he looked closer at the sparkle, he noticed that there was something else in the box. At the bottom was a piece of folded paper. It was a small piece of paper that someone must have put in there many years ago, for the paper was already quite yellowed and felt very old when Tom took it out of the box. As he held it in his hand, he felt the gaze of the dream interpreter once again. Without unfolding the paper, he gave it to him. It was his reward, and Tom had no right to it. The wise old man received it gratefully, unfolded it, and began to read what was written there. The words touched his soul. It was something he did not often experience even as a dream interpreter. He felt the little boy's hand caress his soul as he read those lines.

"Keep it in your heart," said the wise man as he handed the note back to Tom. Tom was surprised. "What am I supposed to do with it now?" He had expected the dream interpreter to keep the paper or reveal an interpretation to him from it. "That, as always, is your decision. Your debt is paid, for you have shown me all I asked for."

Tom looked at the paper, which must have been written on ages ago. Was it a copy of the emerald tablet, the shard of which Tom still possessed? Before he also began to read the lines, the wise man turned to him one last time. "One more request I have, if I may," he said, and Tom asked him to speak.

"Pass on what you have learned. My time on earth is limited. But the world soul always needs someone to show the seekers the way."

Epilogue

Tom closed the book. It had taken him a long time to write everything down. Now he sat in his garden with deep inner peace and listened to the birds. He felt as if he had experienced it all over again. The story of Ala K'in and his donkey in the seemingly timeless desert. A story that concerned one's self, which, when it set out to find meaning in life, first had to get rid of all thoughts. Thoughts that could distract and confuse, and if one failed to capture them, as had happened to Ala K'in at first, could also lead to the abyss. It was dwelling in the moment that had saved Ala K'in, and that was the first requirement for someone to even begin the search for the meaning of their existence. Wandering around on that quest, as Ala K'in had done in the desert, would obviously get one nowhere. In asking for a specific destination, one's self was always thrown back, just as Ala K'in had always found himself with his donkey back under the palm tree from which he had set out. It was only the letting go and the serenity of finding one's destination at some point that moved the self forward to gain clarity on this path. Thus, it was only when Ala K'in trusted that he would not have to find a way out of the desert that he could realize that the meaning of life would only reveal itself. That he had to go deep within himself to find an answer that he had known once before as a young boy. That the only way in life was to follow his heart, as hard as that might be sometimes. Only the little boy he once was could remind him of that truth. As easy as it had been for him when he rode on the donkey back then, it now seemed harder to Tom as a grown man. But it didn't have to be that hard.

That probably was what his father had wanted to tell him. It was more than an answer that Tom had so desperately sought at the beginning. For the answer lay in what Tom had experienced, and in the piece of paper he had read sometime after the dream interpreter had long since disappeared. Tom, too, had smiled. He had remembered. Years later when he had children of his own, he would go into their room at night and tell it to them. It was the story of the boy who rode on a donkey.

About the Book

The sudden death of his father tears Tom's life apart. In faraway Andalusia, fate leads him to Nepanthé, a place without worry. Being there, strange dreams start to show Tom the way to his innermost self.

Tom remembers his childhood dreams and love. He learns about the happiness of the moment and understands why life's journey doesn't need any destinations. But he also experiences dark thoughts, abysses, and even death.

But before the meaning of his existence is revealed to him, this path holds tests to pass by everyone who truly believes in dreams and does everything to fulfill them.

About the Author

Nestor T. Kolee's writing career started with a mystical experience on the coast of the small fishing village of Paternoster in South Africa, which led him to write the story "The Boy and the Donkey" which made readers reflect and rediscover their own dreams.

www.nestorkolee.com